STORIES
FROM
THE
SANDGATE

JAKLİN ÇELİK

TRANSLATED FROM THE TURKISH BY
NANCY ÖZTÜRK

Published by Çitlembik Publications
Şeyh Bender Sokak 18/5 Asmalımescit Tünel
80050 Istanbul TURKEY
Tel: 0 212 292 30 32 / 252 31 63 Fax: 0 212 293 34 66
Web page: www.citlembik.com.tr / www.nettleberry.com
E-mail: kitap@citlembik.com.tr

Translator
Nancy Öztürk

Editor
Amy Spangler

Cover Illustration
Ender Özkahraman

Typesettingy
Tarkan Togo

Printing and Binding by
Berdan Matbaası

ISBN: 975-6663-12-X

THE SANDGATE... KUMKAPI

The historic district of Kumkapı (literally, the Sandgate) lies within the walls of the old city of Istanbul. The district's gate opened onto a ancient port of the Marmara Sea where sand-laden ships used to dock dock in the Byzantine era, hence the name "Sandgate."

After the conquest of the city by the Ottomans in 1492, Sultan Mehmet II brought Armenians into the city, perhaps in an effort to balance the majority Greek Orthodox population, and many of these Armenians were settled in the Sandgate district. The district became an almost entirely Armenian enclave when the seat of the Armenian Patriarchy was moved there in 1641. Today the district still reflects the architectural style of its Greek and Armenian residents and this character is especially evident in its surviving wooden structures. The district is in the process of yet another population shift, however, and is attracting large numbers of Anatolian migrants. The architecture is changing, too, as the traditionally finely crafted, historic homes are rapidly being replaced by unsightly concrete blocks of buildings.

Because of its seaside location, the inhabitants of the district have traditionally worked as fishermen and rowers. Through the centuries the Sandgate has also been noted for its drinking places, tavernas and restaurants kept by its Christian Greek and Armenian inhabitants. This tradition continues and even today its meyhane culture is alive and booming.

The faces of the district are changing, however, as villagers from Turkey's eastern and southeastern provinces have been flocking to the area. Unemployment and social inequities have forced many of the newcomers from their homes in eastern provinces like Diyarbakır, Mardin, Bitlis, and Siirt and many have chosen to settle here in the Sandgate.

The immigration of the past fifty years has also been matched by an emigration. Today very few Armenians remain in the Sandgate. Many of its former Greek residents have moved to Greece while the Armenians have moved to Europe and the USA or to other districts of Istanbul.

Having moved with my family from Diyarbakır to the Sandgate when I was six years old, I grew up in this district. Like most of the other Armenians, my family has also moved on, some to America and Europe and others, like myself, to other parts of the city. But the district lives on in me and these are my stories.

Jaklin Çelik

Contents

HOUSE HUNTING

"This has to be the place", thought the young woman as she stopped in front of the traditional wooden Ottoman house with its jumba, the wide bay windows projecting from the upper floors. She let her eyes slowly take in the four-storeyed house while the little girl clinging tightly to her hand shuddered in amazement at the building's size. After the woman yanked twice on the rope hanging through the doorframe, she and the girl heard a bell sound from within, repeating itself three or four times. The child was dumbfounded and, try as she might, couldn't connect her mother's pulling on the rope with the ringing of the bell. The young woman hurriedly patted her clothes into place and checked once again to make sure that the child's handkerchief was in her pocket.

"Make sure you use your handkerchief if your nose runs."

The child nodded her head in assent, thrusting her hand into her pocket and tightly clutching her handkerchief.

It wasn't long before the huge wooden door opened, first with a "shlink" and then with a "shlank." A long rope hanging from the highest point of the ceiling was attached to the locking mechanism on the door panel. A tug on the rope from the upper floors allowed the door to slide open on its tracks. The first thing the child sensed as the door opened was a whiff of cool air on her face. She was excited with her first peek inside. After they stepped into the high-ceilinged, marble-floored entryway, her mother carefully shut the wooden door. The child heard the door closing with its "shlank" sound.

A double wooden staircase with a graceful bend led from the left and the right to the second floor. Two stone steps followed down between the staircases to two small spaces under the stairwells, both closed off with wooden doors.

The mother and child heard the sounds of someone slowly moving down the stairs.

The young woman guessed that it was the landlady.

Slipping her hand from her mother's grasp, the child stepped down towards the door leading to the garden at the lower left. Her face was struck by rays of sunlight and a smell of must and mold. Then the gleam of a colorful plate caught her eye. But before she could even reach out to touch it, the plate seemed to be on the floor.

From behind her an old and raspy voice cried, "Don't touch that! Look what you've done!"

Her mother's mortified expression was the first thing the child registered. Biting her lower lip, the young woman picked up the plate and carefully put it back, covering once again the clean circle on the dusty shelf. The child finally mastered the courage to look into the face of the old woman, a face just as frightening as her raspy voice. There was nothing soft about this woman, including her body, which seemed hard as stone under her pink dressing gown. Her wrinkled, gray hands trembled. The child immediately knew that this white-haired, cottony-faced woman was displeased with her for she made her dislike of the child very obvious.

The old lady turned towards the young woman who was hunting for a house to rent.

"I won't have a family with children in my house," she sputtered.

Any expression of blame for the child clinging to the hem of her skirt disappeared at once from the young woman's face. It was obvious that the old woman would not accept children in her house and so any attempt at persuasion would be useless. Seeing that this one small child had been enough to instill displeasure, how could she begin to explain to this hard woman that there were yet two more children waiting for her at home, children who had also begged to come along on this house-finding mission.

The brief silence was broken by the soft slap of slippered feet coming down the stairs.

"Dizgin Azat, ur es?"

"Hos em Kayane, yegur!"

The child's eyes opened wide as she listened. The woman speaking that unknown language was getting closer. She stared at the old woman's black net slippers before looking into her face. Kayane turned to Azat, speaking to her in Istanbul-accented Armenian.

"They came about the house?" she asked.

Azat's response gave sound to her displeasure. "Ehhh...."

Kayane turned towards the young woman:

"Are you *Hay*?" she asked, and then tried to reform the question, "I mean to ask if you are Armenian."

The young woman seemed perturbed by the question. "My husband is Hay, but I am Assyrian."

Now it was the turn of the two women to be disconcerted. They looked at the young woman questioningly.

"Does that mean you have been baptized?" asked Kayane.

The young woman was surprised at their question. "Of course, just like all Christians."

The young woman had only come to rent the house and was taken back by the personal questions posed by the older women.

Kayane quickly tried to smooth over the situation.

"Forgive us, Daughter, for our ignorance. Neither I nor Azat have ever met an Assyrian before. Is the boy yours?"

Her kind demeanour softened the tension in the air.

"She's a girl, not a boy," rejoined the young woman.

Kayane's eyes were misty behind her butterfly frame glasses. When she reached down and kissed the girl's cheeks, the musty smell of the house was masked momentarily by an odor of naphthalene mixed with garlic. She turned to the young woman:

"Do you have any other children?"

The answer was hurried. "One older girl and a young son. They're at home."

Kayane turned to Azat, "*Azat ka*, it looks like our house is going to get merry!" Azat's expression was blank as she turned towards Kayane. She was obviously angry.

The young woman quickly began to list her children's good attributes. The little girl took out her handkerchief and quietly wiped her runny nose. As she did so, she stared hard and long into the eyes of the raspy-voiced old woman.

It was thus that the landlady, Azat *Hanım*, reluctantly agreed to rent her house to a family with three children. She also began to recite her own list of requirements.

"The stairs and the entryway will be mopped once a week.

4

The wood has to be wiped with a rag that's been wrung almost dry. A wet rag will rot the stairs. The entry floor is marble so it gets muddy when walked on with wet shoes. The entryway windows facing the street will be cleaned once a month. Cobwebs will be swept away. No slamming the door. And the children can't run down the stairs; they must walk down them slowly. My house is not to be used like a street. Anything else, well, get yourselves settled in and then we'll talk again. That's all I can think of at the moment..."

Kayane turned to her with a pained expression. "Don't scare the girl so. She'll think she's coming here as a maid."

Azat responded with an angry glare.

The young woman was quick to intercede, "That's perfectly all right. I accept those conditions."

Kayane was relieved.

***

Naturally enough, at that point in time, no one could have guessed the later outcome of that first meeting. How could they? Who would have guessed that just five years later Azat, who had been so mean that day, would adopt the young woman as her own daughter or that the young woman would live in that house she was later to inherit, just because of her memories and respect for the old lady.

The easiest thing to predict from that first day was that the little girl and Azat would never, ever mend the hard feelings of that first encounter. And that those first glances between the two would never be erased from the girl's memory, even when, years later, her adoptive-grandmother lay on her deathbed...

5

As for Kayane, she and the little girl would form a tight and loving bond. Later, when she asked the child if she would miss her when she died, the child would not be able to answer. But the girl's answer would come again and again in the years after her untimely death.

But no one knew these things that day....

From now on, the girl was free to go into the garden. Whenever, though, she stepped over the threshold, she would hear again that old and raspy voice:

"Don't step there! You'll track mud in!"

THREE LIGHT,
SWEET SMELLING BREATHS

The big truck lumbered down the hill and turned into the street. It was covered with a shirting of lime and cement that it spread in thick clouds on the asphalt street as it bounced in and out of the potholes. Nevertheless, the truck driver looked strong and adept at maneuvering the heap of the old truck. The wheels revolved slowly while the morning silence of the neighborhood was shattered by the growl of its motor, waking everybody and everything along the street. When the motor was turned off, its exhaust fumes seemed to crawl along and over the windowsills, bringing with their sour smell the threat of an instant headache. The driver opened the door and jumped down while two laborers climbed out on the passenger's side and began to stack shovels and spades and sledge hammers against the wall. The driver climbed back into his truck, engaged the clutch, and started up the engine again. He left in the same direction he had come, again in a cloud of noise and dust and fumes, with first the truck and then the noise dissipating from the street.

A long, long time ago, back when I was a little girl, Anahid *Teyze* would give me slices of bread spread with her homemade preserves. One Mother's Day, I left three carnations along the wall of her house as a thank you for those jams. It is almost as punishment for those happy memories that today those spades and shovels and sledge hammers are propped up against that same wall.

It was obvious that this was the first time these men had been in the streets of the Kumkapı neighborhood. The pair was straight out of a comic book, one of the workers tall and thin, the other short and fat. Each, though, looked like he would be good at his trade and each had black eyes shining from behind thick lashes like night in the middle of the day. The men briefly looked the house over, from top to bottom and bottom to top. Their two or three swift kicks to the locked wooden door, though, proved to be in vain. It refused to open. The door offered up its own resistance to the onslaught, the resistance perhaps stemming from the history of the house itself or perhaps in memory of those who had lived in it. But mostly it was for the years of the house, for the memories that it resisted, for those who had come to and those who had left this house. The resistance was, I think, in memory of those lives lived here in champagne glasses and for those lives lived in struggles of cracked water glasses. If only these walls with all of their faded colors could speak...

I remember from long, long ago, from when I was a child. I remember how Takvor *Amca* would come home with his hands and arms laden and how with just a whistle, and without ever having to touch the bell, the door would be opened for him by Anahid *Teyze*. It seemed that as the door opened, so, too, did her heart; the wings of the door opening onto an endless sky, her passion to unknown depths, her love to eternity... Like pages in

8

a book, with new sentences of promises of new love, each day, every day. Not ones to spend much time out and about amongst the others, it was at this door that everyone would see them. They were known as the happy people of this threshold. Few knew, however, how Anahid *Teyze* had buried her mother the day before her wedding and how she left her father's home in the depths of grief. Or that her happiness was marred by her sorrow the night she stepped over this threshold wearing her wedding gown.

That same night, the blood rose in her and through her. She was proud of her husband as she sent him off in the mornings. And each night and each morning the same, the awakening and the pride. She was filled with him, the pride of him, the sky, the moon, the sun, the body of him. Her body and his body, joined as one. And the child fell from the sky to the womb. The next time Anahid crossed over the threshold she was carrying her daughter Linda in her arms. The door was beautiful. And as noble, she thought, as it was beautiful.

The shorter and fatter of the two workers suddenly left off what he had been doing and began talking to his partner, "My wife is really sick. I want to send her to the village but she wants to go to a doctor. She wears two gold coins around her neck. There's no getting around it; we're going to have to sell them."

He continued trying to work out his problems in his mind. He knew that their lack of money was the actual root of all of their problems. The taller of the two took a pack of cigarettes out of his pocket and offered one to his buddy.

"How many children have you got?"

The shorter inhaled deeply on his cigarette. The question

9

had seemed to stir him out of his quandary, as it was a question he liked.

"Five children!"

His voice had come alive. After a brief pause he took another long drag on his cigarette.

"And three daughters..."

He seemed to have pulled himself together. As was his habit, he spit generously into his right hand and then rubbed both hands together to evenly distribute the sticky substance. He picked up the sledgehammer and hit the door with a powerful blow, once, twice. The wood slowly buckled beneath the hammer. Despite the problems raging within his skull, his face reflected his satisfaction with his physical prowess. The sledgehammer continued to move, up and down, now biting into the wooden stairs. He wondered to himself if they would be able to finish the job today. If they couldn't finish, it would probably mean that they would earn no extra money for the extra day worked. He thought it best not to leave it up to chance. They should finish the job today.

A long, long time ago, way back in my childhood, before the door had this faded color, I would stare at the knots in the wood of the door, letting my mind roam about in the realm of fantasy as I waited for it to be opened upon my knock. I would gaze at the panels of the door, imagining that each of these was a tree growing in a dark and dense forest. A strong wind would blow and then these trees would swing to the left and to the right, opening up a road for me alone. When would the wind begin to blow? It was when Anahid *Teyze* would open the door for me, and when the door would give way so that I could enter this house.

The walls of the curved staircase were decorated with beautiful oil paintings. Three depicted women, women who were fine and elegant and beautiful. It was evident that these were women who were valued and loved. Anahid *Teyze* also respected these women. Takvor *Amca*'s grandfather had had them painted. Who could guess what memories lay in these paintings.

The shorter of the two men now set to work with his chisel, peeling the paint off the walls, layer by layer. The image of a woman's long and slender throat, swanlike and adorned with a necklace, seemed to gradually take form on the wall as he worked. It reminded him of his wife Rendihan and her throat adorned with the gold coins. Couldn't he find some way not to sell them? His mind was occupied with these thoughts as he finished the first floor stairs. He looked again at the throat of the headless and bodiless woman. "Rendihan," he whispered. They were now at the jumba floor.

I climbed slowly up the stairs. No one else was there. The breeze seemed to caress the faces of the three women as I continued on my way to the jumba floor. The women's cheeks were red with blush. They seemed embarrassed but proud at the same time.

How Anahid *Teyze* and Takvor *Amca* loved to sit in the broad bay window - the jumba - drinking their coffee and conversing. The best time was Sunday evenings, with the window looking out onto the sunset and the angels in the lace curtains floating lightly in the breeze. All who sat here marvelled at the angel design worked into the curtains. The jumba windows were swathed from ceiling to floor in these long, cream-colored crocheted curtains. Above the jumba was the small balcony with its iron railings sporting roses and vines. It was on this small balcony that Anahid *Teyze* dried Linda's diapers and tiny clothes.

The workers had smashed their way up to the balcony. The short one swung away with his cutting tool, puncturing the iron railings. Soon the iron gave way to tin.

"There's tin at the base."

"Whatever. May Allah help us and not make this job harder than it is."

It was almost time for the sun to reach its highest point. The sun reflected off their faces. As they blinked their eyes in the heat and the sun, a few of their thick black lashes floated down to the street below.

"If we can get the jumba knocked down, the job'll be over before seven. We can dust ourselves off and call it a day by six at the latest."

There was one more flight of stairs to go and then they were on the roof terrace.

Flowerpots lined the low wall encircling the terrace. Pots with roses and oleanders and four o-clocks: yellow, red, purple, white, sentries for violet evenings spent on the terrace. It was there on purple nights that the most beautiful of songs were sung, with never before discovered notes. Notes that rose to greet the night stretching out before them and were then written in the notebooks of the sky. They drank *rakı* as they sat on the terrace gazing at the sea below and beyond. The lights from the ferryboats seem to compete with the starlight as the *rakı* bottle grew empty. The fragrance of the oleander and the four o-clocks mingled with the sweet licorice aroma of the *rakı*. And Takvor *Amca*'s heart seemed to break with the beauty of that night. He inhaled three light, sweet-smelling breaths.

The first was the liquorice as the *rakı* glass dropped from his hand just as he was taking his last swallow.

The second was the oleander, its fragrance absorbed into his body.

The third was the rose: "Anahid," he whispered as his head came to rest alongside Anahid's favorite pot of roses.

And that was his end, his final defeat in spite of himself and everything. His body sagged, falling onto the concrete of his beloved terrace.

Anahid *Teyze*'s body was wrapped in black clothes and her face in sorrow as we sat in the jumba. She told me that Takvor Amca had gone off to a far away place. She said she was sad because he had not taken her with him and that is why she wore black. I was so mad at Takvor *Amca*. I made the sign of the cross as I vowed that the next time he came from the market, I wouldn't help him carry his sacks.

"Okay, this is the spot," said the shorter and the fatter of the two workers as he started to hammer away at the spot where Takvor Amca had fallen. The concrete moaned. The tiles, asleep for so many years, tried to withstand the sharp blows as they drew even tighter together. The joys and the sorrows, the lives that were lived here and those cut short, the days, and the months, and the years. For all of these the tiles held tight. But the bonds slowly gave way and, before long, they had dismantled the terrace. The jumba floor was now unroofed with the floor left naked and exposed to the sky above. I wonder if it is only people who are unneedingly ashamed of their nakedness, or if houses feel the same shame, too?

It started when Anahid sent her daughter off as a bride to France. With all the sensitivity of her womanness, she tried to cling to her memories in this house. Later, longing to see her first grandchild, she sold the house as she left for France, never to return.

The terrace was now empty. It seemed like a thousand years had passed since those dry pots had held flowers. The sky in its beauty had cut off all relations with the terrace, the floor of which was now covered with seagull filth and pigeon feathers. The breeze had deserted the terrace as well and no longer beckoned me to play. I was hurt, but even more than that, I was angry. I wanted to scream as loudly as I possibly could.

"When they come back I will never, ever carry Takvor *Amca*'s bags and I will never, ever again eat Anahid *Teyze*'s preserves."

My anger and my screams invited the breeze. But nothing and nobody turned an ear to my longing - not the breeze, nor the others. Not that day, not ever.

It was five o'clock and they were getting tired. It was just an ordinary close of day, no different from any other. And they shook the dust off of themselves.

"I'm not going to send her," said the shorter of the two. The taller one didn't understand.

"I'm not going to send Rendihan to the village. And I'm not going to sell her coins. That necklace looks nice around her throat."

THE SEA FOR MIGIRDIÇ
AND
THE SKY FOR SARKIS

Mıgırdıç was upset as he left home that morning. Even before he could shut the door, his wife Vartuhi's low growly voice had caught him by the collar:

"Mıgırdiiiiiç, midyanerı mendz u makrıvadz ıllan."

It just couldn't be so! When he married her fifty years ago, her voice had been so sweet, so clear. But now, when she reminded Mıgırdıç that the mussels should be both large and clean, it was as though she were stuttering. Who could have guessed back then that such a change could happen?

Varturi's arteries were hardening. Each year her memory became a little weaker and she forgot more and more often what she said and how she should act. Last New Year's she even forgot to add the tiny currants to her stuffed mussels. In point of fact, she had even forgotten that Mıgırdıç was a fisherman. In years past, it was enough just to say the word "mussel," but now, she just didn't know what to do.

The reason why Mıgırdıç was upset as he left this morning was that he just could not tolerate her constant repetitions any longer. Vartuhi always seemed to catch him before he had the

15

chance to shut the door, before he could get across the threshold. Her lips, covered in a thick lipstick, would draw back and pull towards her ears as she continued,

"Don't you hear me? Look at that, he doesn't even bother to answer me, his wife! But he knows enough how to slurp up the mussels when he has them in front of him!"

And then, one by one, she would begin to open each dirty page of their lives.

"*Kavuy*, let them pee on my head, I thought he had some shit to him. My God, if I had known. If only I had married that Garo, think of what my life would be like today!"

Actually, Mıgırdıç knew that Vartuhi didn't really mean what she said. But still it hurt him. The fifty years they had shared together. And now she would trade him for someone she would never have thought of marrying, trade him even for some stuffed mussels.

"Oh, if only that New Year's hadn't been so cold and snowy," he thought to himself.

That New Year's he was only in his twenties, a young man in his very young prime. He was alone in Istanbul... No mother, no father.

He stopped under a streetlight in front of the Armenian Bezciyan School. As he watched all of the people getting ready to welcome in the New Year, he felt lonely to the very core of his soul, and suddenly began to sob loudly. The tears streaming down his face melted the snowflakes that dripped down to his collar.

He hit his head against the post.

"Oh, this loneliness."

He remembered with a smile now his longing then for a wife and someone to share the New Year with.

16

As he tried to shrug off his long ago memories, he thought to himself, "So this is what my fate had in store for me."

He shrugged with annoyance at himself. "Couldn't I have found some other post to hit my head on? My God Mıgırdıç, what has happened has happened, what's over is over..."

He could almost taste the stuffed mussels as he turned to Vartuhi, "Have we got currants at home? Do you want me to bring some on the way back?"

"Zo, have you gone senile? Can you think I wouldn't have currants? Just like there's no sea without fish, there's no house without currants."

Mıgırdıç sighed deeply and set off.

"My God, Garo, you might be dead and buried now but still you were lucky not to get this. Oh, those long ago days! God, Mıgır, has the sea gone dry or have you dried up the sea in seventy years? No, no, I may not know nothing, but I know for sure that living with this woman has changed me into a shriveled-up, dried-up fish. It won't be long now till they lay the old fisherman on the bier at the Balıklı Graveyard."

He felt a hand on his shoulder. He turned to get a look at the owner of the hand, his best friend, the blacksmith Sarkis. It was obvious from his labored breathing that Sarkis had run to catch up with him. Without even breaking to say hello, Mıgırdıç continued with the thoughts he was meshing over in his brain, this time putting them into words.

"The sea at Kumkapu is a puddle for her! That woman would dry up an ocean! And all the fish in it! And still she wouldn't admit it was her doing!"

"Who are you talking about?"

"Who else, Vartuhi, that's who!"

Sarkis still didn't understand. He was almost completely deaf now.

"What happened to Vartuhi?"

Mıgırdiç decided against describing the events of the morning. All of a sudden, it was as though he could feel the cobblestones of the street biting into his feet. It was hot, and a warm curtains blowing out of the jumba window. Suddenly, there was a coolness in the air.

"I was talking about the sea. But what do you know of the sea? You're a man of iron, what would you know about water?"

Sarkis had hardly heard a word said, so he just pretended to be able to follow the conversation.

"Yeah, our water is cut off too, but we're making do with the cistern."

"You don't even know what the sea smells like, Sarkis! You've been pounding hot iron so long, you don't even have a sense of smell anymore. Your nose works no better than your ears. Anyway, what do you know of mussels, of clams?"

"What made you think about my Grandpa's hundred head of cattle in Bolu? It was when they all got that sickness that my grandfather got sick, too, and went with them to the grave."

His face became bathed in sorrow, just like it did every other time he told this story.

"What I'm trying to say is that the cattle just turned traitor on us. One thing's for sure, iron work won't betray a man. The trade was handed down to me from my father. But what would you know of iron? Every word you say has to smell of the sea."

"You're making things up again Sardis. I didn't say 'calves,' I said 'clams.' Vartuhi asked me for clams for tonight."

"Are you out of your mind, Man? *Meğa Asdudzo!*"

exclaimed Sarkis as he raised his eyes towards the heavens. "Now he thinks his wife is a clam."

He turned to Mıgırdiç, "You know what? Mine's more like a *lüfer*. But each to his own, right?" he added with a broad wink.

They walked along the shore until settling into one of old Salih's chairs at his tea stand. Salih walked over and said to Mıgırdiç, "Let me bring you a glass of tea before you start watering the sea with your tears."

Mıgırdiç's eyes had already misted over. How hard this getting old was. Two drops of tears formed over the seaweed-bound irises of his eyes and as they slowly wound down the course of his deeply wrinkled skin, skin deeply tanned by sun and sea and wind, he raised his hand to wipe them away and then gave up, letting them make their way down to his chin. After all, the tears seemed to wash away the sand of his dreams. When he wiped them, they seemed only to beget more water, and the salt begat salt while waves wiped across his cheeks.

His eyes swept out and into the sea, drawing a line between the water and his desire. He breathed in a sigh deep with longing and then remembered that Sarkis was there with him.

As Salih brought the tea to the table, "Whoops, I'm late with the tea again. Stop that, please, Mıgırdiç."

Mıgırdiç looked first at his watch and then at the sun.

"Oh my son, Salih, what kind of luck is this for me? At home I have a forgetful wife and out of the house a deaf friend!"

Sarkis read the expression on his friend's face:

"Okay," he said, "It's a deal. The sea is yours and the sky is mine!"

In order to cheer him up, he gave his friend a gift of the thing he loved most, and at the same time, took a share of the sky for himself.

Mıgırdiç was pleased with the gift and with the sudden gesture of generosity, but how to communicate this to a friend who could not hear him out?

He chose his words carefully and enunciated them as clearly as possible:

"I swear that this sky of yours has been witness to all of our stormy love-making, as I have been witness to the sea and the waves. The day is coming - not far off I think - that when I die — let this sky of yours be my witness — I have no desire for the black earth. You may accept the ground that your grandfather lies in, you may even accept the sparks flying off the molten iron, but I, no, I can never accept them. Let it be known that the place I lie - whether it should happen sooner or later - should be the place where the waves can beat over me. Let your sky be my witness, I want seagulls to be my angels of death."

WOMEN'S WARD

"Uhh, sorry to bother you, but I want to pass out cigarettes to the women on the ward in remembrance of the souls of my loved ones who have passed away," said the young woman.

The thick black jacket and the red woolen scarf she wore tightly wound around her head barely protected her from the cold outside. But now, inside, she was hot and the extra clothing had become a burden and the long wait indoors was making her even more uncomfortable.

The nurse's aide was used to people coming in to hand out cigarettes in memory of a loved one, but this case was different. Most of those people were at least forty or older and many used this act as a way to repent for a sin or to make up for whatever was bothering them. This woman, though, was much younger than the typical repenter.

She closed the small iron grille and began to unlock the door.

"Okay, come on in," she said.

The young woman was pleased to think that the sun chose not only to shine on goat tenders like herself, but also generously awarded its soothing rays to those non-goat tending souls as well. "So," she asked herself, "what have we done to drive these people out of their minds?" Of course, it was said to be a condition ordained by God, but still it seemed that this group could be divided into two categories: those that God had decided to punish with this kind of affliction from birth, and those that became like this later. Even God must look down in amazement at this second group. These people, after all, were sickened by man's own willingness to play with others as if they are pieces of a jigsaw puzzle. Their degree of illness correlates directly to the severity of events they were forced to experience, events played out by mothers and fathers, brothers and sisters, and children, so that this kind of oppression emerges as a kind of infection of life, an infection eating away at the very core of life. And then the law gives us the right to play some more with the puzzle and move these people again across the line and summarily deposit them here. The basic problem remains of course: this is a dance of partners.

The women heard the door open and close and so began to come out of their rooms, singly and in pairs. One by one they approached the young woman to shake her hand or kiss her cheeks and hug her as if they had been friends forever. Most were old and overweight. Many had excess facial hair that had grown almost into beards. Most stared absently into space and spoke slowly with disjointed words that didn't combine in a way that made obvious sense.

The young woman opened her plastic bag and began taking out Samsun and Maltepe brand cigarettes. The tight circle around her began to loosen as she handed out the packs. Suddenly, she found herself staring into the eyes of Hayguhi, a woman standing on the periphery of the circle and looking at her intensely.

Hayguhi appeared to be about thirty years old. She had just combed her hair, which was short but not shorn like the other patients. The eyeliner she had used accentuated her every look. Her eyes were obsidian, shiny and sharp. Her grooming made it seem as if she were momentarily expecting a visitor. Next to her stood Arşaluys, another young woman in her early thirties. Arşaluys' face, though, was pinched and pale and her eyes reflected that dull and absent stare so common here. Her body seemed to be in constant motion, as if she were readying herself to perform some act.

A cacophony of sound issued from the rooms along the corridor, voices that rose and fell with seemingly no relation to one another, voices strident with laughter and cursing. The young woman had emptied the bag. She began to walk along the corridor, this time accompanied by Hayguhi and Arşaluys. She could answer most of their questions simply with a nod or shake of her head as she turned her eyes to look at the women in their rooms. The three then sat down on a bench under the window at the end of the corridor. She felt around in her pocket. Yes, her small tape recorder was still there. Arşaluys suddenly thrust her hand into the pocket also and pulled out the recorder.

"This is mine now. You gave it to me, didn't you?"

"No, I didn't. I can't."

"This is a recorder and I want to listen to music!"

The young woman took the recorder from Arşaluys' hands and put it back into her pocket.

"It's not a tape recorder. It's a telephone."

Now Hayguhi's interest was piqued.

"Can I make a phone call?"

"Not this time, but the next time, promise. Who did you want to call?"

"Don't you know I have a daughter? She's eleven now. I want to call her."

Arşaluys broke in, "She doesn't have any daughter! She doesn't have a husband either. Can somebody have a daughter if she hasn't got a husband? Besides, that's not a telephone. That's a tape recorder. Only somebody as crazy as you would believe that's a telephone."

"This is a telephone but right now it doesn't work because there's no network in this area."

Arşaluys was getting angry and so walked away mumbling to herself.

The young woman spoke softly to Hayguyi, "I believe you have a daughter. And since you are her mother, she must also be a very nice and very pretty girl."

Hayguhi was happy again. She took a lipstick out of her purse and freshened up her bright red lips.

"I want to get out of here. I don't want to stay here any-more. I want you to help me get out of here."

"I would like to, really, but I can't. There's nothing I can do."

"What's it like out there? It's nice, isn't it? Tell me what it's like out there."

Wasn't it time for her to leave? She was beginning to be overwhelmed with demands she couldn't meet and questions that had no rational base.

"The outside is no different from this! Forget about it. Being here is actually better than being out there."

She suddenly understood that this new and fragile friendship was being shattered. Hayguhi made a move to walk away, but then stopped. The expression of her eyes changed. Now they shone with reflected anger. Her conversational tone changed as well. The friendliness was gone and replaced by clipped and clearly spoken words.

"You're lying. You're nothing but a liar. A very bad liar. You live a life of ease out there. You drink tea when you want tea. You go where you want to go. Why didn't you think to bring me a hot cup of tea? I have been here eight years and in those eight years I have never met a worse liar than you!"

"No, Hayguhi, I am telling you the truth. Outside is no different from inside. I have been outside for twenty-eight years, so I should know."

"Are you sure you're telling me the truth?"

The young woman started to speak of the outside world.

Hayguhi had a different perspective on everything. The young woman told her very personal things, true things. But was this the right person to be telling these things to?

Suddenly Arşaluys reappeared, aide in tow. Arşaluys seemed to be skipping down the corridor, waving her arms, speaking fast, "In her pocket. It's in her pocket!"

The aide was brusque, "Let's see what you've got in your pocket."

"Sure enough," she replied following the aide towards the office.

"Yes, I've got a tape recorder in my pocket. But I didn't turn it on. I didn't record anyone."

"How dare you do such a thing! Don't you know that I would be fired if they found out?"

"I'm sorry. Look, if you want, I can take out the tape and give it to you."

25

Arşaluys was behind them.

"I fooled you. I fooled you. It's not a tape recorder. It's a telephone."

"See, she says it's a telephone."

"What does it matter what she says? She's crazy. She can say anything. If she tells the doctor, I'll lose my job."

The young woman spoke to Arşaluys, making her voice sound as strict and serious as possible.

"Look, the thing in my pocket is a telephone."

"The thing in your pocket is a tape recorder!"

She emptied her eyes, modelling them on the distant eyes of Arşaluys and turned her gaze on the young patient.

"No, it's a telephone."

"Tape recorder."

"Telephone."

"Recorder."

"Telephone."

"Recorder!"

"Telephone!"

Arşaluys slid her eyes from the grasp of the young woman and turned to the aide.

"Yes, it's a telephone."

"A telephone, right?"

"Sure, a telephone."

She turned on her heels and left. The aide was obviously surprised by the exchange.

"If you want, I'll give you the cassette."

"That's OK, ten minutes later they get their meal. You've got to leave anyway."

She followed Arşaluys into her room where Arşaluys now lay

huddled on her bed. The young woman planted a kiss on her cheek.

"What does it matter? Telephone. Tape recorder. Come on, let's make up."

"Only if you promise to come again."

"Of course I will. I promise."

They were soon joined by Hayguhi and then the three began to walk together towards the door. Here each of the patients hugged the young guest, planting kisses on her cheeks.

Hayguhi had a question. "I want to ask you something, but you've got to promise to tell me the truth." She turned to the young woman and looked her full in the face with her large brown eyes. "Look in my eyes. Do they have an empty look to them? Tell me the truth."

"No, Hayguhi, your eyes are not empty. In fact, you have the prettiest eyes on the ward."

RECKONING WITH THE MAKER

Necla had passed out in the taxi again, just as she did every night. It was just as she felt the car turning into her street that she started to come to. The taxi stopped in front of the burned-out hulk of the wooden house next to the modern apartment building. The back door opened. The quiet of the night was suddenly shattered by Necla's deep-throated and now slurred voice.

"You've loved too, but you're a man. Anyway, *Abi* don't take this personal, but all men..."

"Okay, okay, *Abla* take your change and get into your house before you get all wet. Come on, *Abla*, don't keep me waiting now; I've got to put up with all this shit, too, just to earn my day's bread."

Necla was set on not getting out of the car.

"It's not like I don't work too! I do, from morning to night. But do I complain? God knows you're probably married and got three kids to boot. Keep the change."

Necla's insistent conversations with the taxi drivers were repeated every night. It was just this driver's luck that on this

28

particular night, she seemed quite determined to keep the talk going. Necla took a bottle of perfume out of her purse and thrust it towards the driver.

"Take this and give it to your wife."

"Forget it, *Abla*, put it back in your purse."

Necla's eyes became saddened in a curiously guilty manner as they grew smaller and smaller in the middle of her face, wrinkled beyond her years. She was insistent.

"*Abi*, I know I look dirty. I know your wife is probably cleaner than me. Come on, don't jazz me. Take this home to your wife."

As she said this, her voice once again took on its former growly tone. The driver was anxious to get rid of her, so he took the bottle from her hand and put it in the glove compartment. Necla stepped out of the car. Then just as she was about to shut the door, the lights to the apartment building staircase suddenly lit up. The light reflected off the yellow of the taxi. In no time, the janitor Satılmış appeared at the building's front door.

"Come on Miss Necla, come on inside. Let the driver go home now."

Necla was now out of the car and had slammed its door.

"What's it to you? What's it to you what time I get home? And what are you doing outside at this hour? Why did you crawl out of your wife's warm arms? Why aren't you in there making more babies? After all, God has given you a bed and a mate just as he gives you food for your body."

Necla made two fists and hit one hand over the other in the universal gesture.

"Come on, Miss Necla, we've always treated you nice. We call you '*Abla*.' We've never failed to show you respect. But now you're taking things too far. You can go to hell and back for all I care."

Satılmış's voice had lost all pretence of civility and now echoed the true feelings he was unleashing.

Necla was pleased to have evoked this kind of response from the janitor.

"Look here you faggot! Every time I come home you start smelling around my doorstep just like a cat in front of a butcher's shop. I wish to hell that God damns the very soles of your feet!"

Lightening had struck. Satılmış's face was now a sick and pearly shade of white.

"You whore!"

"I'll show you who's the whore around here!"

Necla walked to the front of the burned-out house. She pulled up her skirt and pulled down her underpants and, standing, started to pee against the charred frame.

Satılmış watched her pee mix with the rainwater at the curbside. His eyes were large with shock.

"Faggot!"

He turned around and walked back to the apartment building. His wife was waiting for him at the door.

"What the hell are you doing out here? Get back in the house!"

He grabbed his wife's arm and pulled her into the building with him.

His voice carried out into the street as he shut the building door, "She used to be a whore, but now she's become a fag."

When Necla turned around, she realized that the taxi was gone.

It seemed that the rain had stopped as well. She began beating on the barred windows of the basement apartment. A light came on from within and then the window opened.

"What are you doing out there at this hour of the night? Don't you know how to come through a door? God give you sense, Necla!"

The woman's head was level with Necla's feet.

"Füsun, look, the rain has stopped. Come on, make us a coffee. I'll drink mine here and you drink yours there."

Necla was back in the swing of things. She called after Füsun who was on her way to the kitchen: "Don't put too much coffee in the pot. I want to read our fortunes. You put too much coffee in and our fortunes always come out black. Do you hear me?"

There was no answer and, anyway, Necla hadn't really expected one. She took off her shoes and, not giving an instant's thought to the rain-soaked pavement, sat down on the sidewalk, dangling her legs through the iron bars of the open window. Five minutes later Füsun was back with their coffees.

"You must have been sound asleep," she told Füsun.

"Why, did I miss something?"

"Well, I really gave old Satılmış a hard time."

The thought of it made her explode into laughter.

"Füsun, you know what? He called me a whore!"

Füsun joined in on the laughter. She placed the saucer down over the cup and rotated it three times before turning it over to have her fortune read.

"Füsun, it's just not fair. Every night it's the same old thing. Doesn't a woman have the right to come home at this time of the night? I am really, truly sick to death of this! Okay, all right, I know I made a little bit of noise, but when a man does the same thing, everybody thinks he's a real man, but when a woman does it, well, then they think she's nothing but a whore. God in heaven, I ask You, is this fair? You made us, You made all of us, didn't You consider what was going to happen?"

She suddenly felt the rain dropping onto her head and over her face. It had started up again. She pulled her legs out of the window and stood up, sticking her feet into her shoes. Füsun was both laughing and trying to talk to Necla at the same time.

"Why blame the Maker? His justice has always been for women and for men. Look around you; nobody else is complaining. Actually, He is the one who is surprised by all of this. How could He guess that the man He made would turn himself into a woman? Anyway, come inside now and let's sit down and drink a double vodka, man to man this time..."

FAN BLADES

The man was startled by a rhythmic noise sounding in his ears.

"...tik-tik, tik-tik..."

He began to toss about in his bed. Emerging slowly out of the depths of sleep, he tried to ascertain the source of the irritating noise, scouring his brain as if it were something he once knew but had forgotten. What could it be? He had failed to come up with an answer, when it occurred to him that maybe the noise was trying to hide itself somewhere in the dream he had been having. As he sensed the first yellow rays of the morning reflecting against the shade on his window, though, he realized that the sound couldn't be emanating from any dream.

"...tik-tik, tik-tik..."

The noise was coming from outside, from the street, from a place nearby. As he still tried to figure out where the sound was coming from, it became more and more buried in some unknown depths.

"...tik-tik, tik-tik..."

He finally climbed out of bed and walked over to the window where he looked out onto the street. Other than the unsettling, rhythmic noise, it seemed to be a typical early Sunday morning.

"...tik-tik, tik-tik, tik-tik..."

He took a deep breath. Then, in that early morning light, just as he had decided to go down to the street to have a look around, he spotted a child in front of the shoe repair shop across the street. His was a tiny body, thin and weak, wrapped in old cast-offs.

In his hands the boy clutched a box of glue, the kind of glue used in the shoe repair shop. His lips seemed to be stuck to the top of the tin. Each time the child breathed in the vapors from the box, his lungs made a "tik" sound, and then a second "tik" came when he exhaled back into the tin.

One of his shoes lay nearby. It appeared that the child had no control over the lower half of his body, as though his legs were disconnected from his torso.

The man realized that the tiny body was pressing down on the child's heart, sticking to it like glue and hindering him from inhaling. That tiny, virtually imperceivable sound that had interrupted his Sunday sleep, would have been drowned out by the cacophony of noises coming from the street on any ordinary day, but now seemed to be charging his ears with all of the disturbing sounds of the world.

"...tik-tik, tik-tik, tik-tik..."

The sound was accompanying him down into the depths of a bottomless shaft and with its every echo, it became more and more difficult for him to exit the shaft. He was drowning.

As the child struggled to his feet, the man himself also stirred a bit. That puny body tottered to the left and to the right, so that it seemed the boy might find himself crashing into the asphalt at any moment. His eyes were only half-open, but his pupils were open wide, reflecting an expression both vacant and cloudy. He could no longer stand up and so he slowly slid back to the ground. The boy then proceeded to retrieve his shoe and crawl, ever so slowly, to the opposite side of the street. In order to get a better look at him, the man leaned out as far as he could, his torso hanging out of the open window. The boy started to fiddle with something at the windows, protected by iron security bars, of the restaurant next door. From his position, the man couldn't see what the boy was trying to do. He seemed to be playing with something. The man thought that perhaps the child was doing something dangerous. He suddenly thought that perhaps the child was trying to light a match and this thought threw the man into a panic. He considered calling the police but then decided this wouldn't be fair to the child. The man felt ashamed that he could have even briefly considered turning this poor child over to the police. He decided that the best thing for him to do would be to go down and investigate for himself.

The child had thrust the fingers of his right hand through the bars and raised his head towards the heavens. He wore a strange smile upon his face. It was a smile that was as mature as that of an old man and as awkward as that of a young child.

It wasn't long before he again hauled up his feather-light body and crawled across the road. He picked up his glue can again and then dragged it across the cobblestones of the sidewalk as he turned the corner. The noise of the can hitting the stones soon melted away. And then again that damned noise, which seemed to have a century of familiarity for the man, began to fill up the very cells of his body.

"Tik-tik!"

The man climbed back into bed, pulling his covers up over his head. The bed had cooled off. He felt safe again as he held his breath, his body warming up from the lack of air. The over-riding need for sleep began at his eyelids and then slowly travelled down, until his body surrendered.

When he awoke around noon, his body was stiff from carry-ing the load of a long, drawn-out dream. He could remember bits and pieces of something, but was unable to complete that jigsaw puzzle of dream and reality, to fit them together to make a comprehensible whole.

Then he began to remember the events of the morning. Again sounds from outside were filling the room, but this time they were the ordinary sounds of an ordinary Sunday. He felt better when he decided that the strong reaction he had experienced in the morning must have been due to his not having fully awakened. The man was enlivened by the sounds coming from the street.

He got out of bed thinking that it would be a good idea to get a start on the day, tossed on his clothes, and stepped out into the street. He was just about to exit the street when he turned back and stood in front of the steel bars on the restaurant window. He noticed that the blades of the exhaust fan in the window turned very slowly, with little help from rare occasional visits from the wind. He stuck his index finger through the bars and gave the plastic blade a few turns. He lifted his head towards the sky, closed his eyes, and continued to turn the blades with his index finger. On his face appeared an expression that gave away his age; it was the smile of a middle-aged man.

THE SAFETY PIN

Spring was the season and May the month; Saturday the day and five o'clock the hour. The air of this season was the kind that sent waves of love and longing coursing through the veins. This longing was so tangible that it even found its way into the blood of fifty-five year old Onnik, Onnik, the one and only son of his loving mother, Onnik, with his five foot five frame, his eggplant nose, and pale and pasty skin, but a face that, all things considered, was not that *kaknem* Onnik knelt before the sacred picture of Jesus.

"And am I to finally see this day? Thanks be to God!"

His mother pushed herself out of her chair, shoving her son aside from the picture as she took her place in the spot. Her raised eyebrows seemed to soften as she spoke in a quiet voice, "*Hisus Kristosus...* Please take my soul now so that I do not have to witness the close of such a day. Let me have taken my last breath before my Onnik comes back to this house."

Onnik's mother was angry with him. It wasn't enough that he had spent the last seven years chasing behind the skirts of that jezebel Yerçanik, but now this very night he was going to take

37

her to the opera!

Onnik had pleaded with his mother to take the suit they had bought eighteen years ago and put away for his marriage out of the armoire where it was stored. His pleas fell on deaf ears. His mother had not accepted any possible candidates for him and it was highly unlikely that she would deign to give her okay to Yerçanik now.

Yerçanik's eyes were slightly crossed and she was on the plump side, but she was from a cultured family. She herself had been unable to attract any man who met her cultural standards. This night was of the greatest importance for Onnik for he and Yerçanik would sit side by side (and perhaps even knee-to-knee) and watch an opera performance. Yesterday he had gone to the bank and exchanged all his banknotes for brand new notes. And, for the love of Jesus, his mother had finally been persuaded to take out the suit from its mothball bag in the closet. After squeezing to death two bedbugs he spotted crawling on the suit, he also located a belt that was in the last stages of its life. It turned out that the belt was too wide for the *britlerine* but he found a solution to this problem as well. Instead of using the belt, he gathered the extra material at the waist of the trousers into a large knot on the right side and held it together with the biggest safety pin he could find. The shoulders of the jacket drooped a bit but there was nothing he could do about that. He combed his hair straight back with lemon water, further accenting his dark brows and large nose. Most reluctantly, his mother finally took out the bottle of cologne that had belonged to her beloved husband and with trembling hands gave two quick swipes of spray to his suit. His carefully polished shoes were placed at the door. He put them on, made the sign of the cross, and remembered to pass over the threshold right foot first. Because she couldn't bear to see her son leave the house, his mother turned her back at his departure.

Yerçanik lived three streets away. Onnik walked with straight legs so as not to make creases at the knees of his trousers. By the time he reached her street, he had already bent down six times to wipe away any dust on his shoes, using the lower part of his inner jacket lining. His heart beat with joy as his shoes stepped lightly on the cobblestones of the street. He unbuttoned his jacket, slipped his hands into his trouser pockets and peered into a shop window to get a reflection of how he looked with this pose. The reflection set him back a bit.

There was a bulge where the safety pin held the cloth. Perhaps he shouldn't put his hands in his pockets? Come on, the pose made him look jaunty. But the bulge! He found a vacant corner and quickly removed the pin. This time he gathered the material at the back of his waist and held it together with the pin. It didn't look nice without the jacket, but, anyway, he wasn't planning on taking the jacket off. He went back to the store window to check out his reflection. This time it looked fine. Especially with his hand in his left pocket.

He set off again. When the toe of his shoe scraped against a cobblestone he worried about ruining the shine but decided to forget about it. He turned into her street. When he saw the curtain at the window on the first floor move a bit he thought his heart might stop. He rang the bell and waited about three and a half minutes for the door to be opened. Finally, the dried-up woman of his dreams opened the door to the waiting, dried-up man. They shook hands. After shaking her hand, Onnik had no idea whatsoever where he should next put his hand. This was the time, he thought, so he thrust his hand into his pocket. Okay, he had done this part all right as well. Onnik flagged down a passing cab and opened the door. Yerçanik stumbled a bit as she was getting into the car; her heavy body had lowered the shocks and she tripped back, stepping on his foot. She apologized profusely, but Onnik was actually somewhat pleased by what had happened. When they arrived at the Opera House, Onnik got out of the cab first and walked around the car to open her door with a gesture reflecting both great patience and exuberance. Yerçanik made no sign of appreciating the attention.

They made small talk till the start of the opera. Though Onnik was trying to bait her towards talk of marriage, Yerçanik completely ignored that course of the conversation. The scene of confession of love and affection he had so carefully contrived was interrupted abruptly by the opening of the stage curtains. Onnik spent the first act trying to determine the exact location of Yerçanik's hand. His own was sweating profusely. His excitement had still not abated. He had been waiting for this minute for seven years now and he spent the next fifteen minutes of the first act planning for the next seven years. He thrust his hand into his pocket and took out his heart medicine. He carefully placed one of the pills under his tongue and then settled back into the chair.

It was at that very instant that the safety pin opened and sunk deep into his backbone. With the bite of the pin his spirit seemed to soar towards the ceiling of the stage, trying to escape through a light fixture but not finding a path. A scream he dared not allow to find voice also fought to escape from his body, following his soul to the rafters. He thought his eyes must surely have popped out of his head and fire seemed to be emanating from his face and his body. Although now dislodged from the bone, the safety pin continued to constitute a dangerous entity for his lower body. Yerçanik hadn't noticed that anything had happened. Just at this moment, Yerçanik's purse slipped from her lap to the floor. Onnik bent down, picked up the purse and handed it to Yerçanik but as soon as he tried to sit back once again the pin made another sharp jab into his flesh about an inch above the first.

My God! What pain! Twice he had to bite his lip to keep the scream from exploding from within him. He held himself as tight as he could until he was almost frozen into place. The pain whirled about inside him until it transformed itself into a bolt of gas that exploded out of his body with a sudden force. My God! Humiliation and extreme embarrassment barrelled him to his feet. He no longer cared a whit about Yerçanik. He ran to the door, feeling the bullet-like stares of the audience pummel at his back.

From that day on, his mother added a second candle to the one she lit every day for her husband in St. Mary's Church.

STATION TRILOGY I

Station Departures: A Life

The new day, preparing itself to take over the city in small encroachments, is heralded in by the first early morning movements of the secretly awakening Kumkapı train station, a station near the downtown end of Istanbul's European-side commuter line. The white rays of sunlight, newly awoken to warm the world, meet with the waves, come to themselves a bit more in those wee hours, and reach the station. The waves swallow up the first yellow reflections of the sun with unexpected agility only to release them as white bubbles; they toss themselves forward in impatience before withdrawing, each time growing a little lazier.

The sound of the train acts as a beacon of its imminent arrival, catalyzing the slow movement into determined activity. The two headlights, its two eyes, seem to pull the giant body with them as they draw nearer at great speed. The brakes screech as the train nuzzles up to the ramp. The train comes to a stop. Before it can straighten up the messy sound it has emitted, it is off again. As it picks up speed, it gradually becomes a small dot in the distance. It once again turns the morning over to the care of a deserted ramp and the sound of singing birds.

I let my eyes roam over the treetops. I seem to play hide and seek with the birds. And then my eyes lock onto the sea.

The night fishing boats are making their way back to land. During the return trip, the nets are being cleaned as happy folk songs glide off the tongues of the fishermen. All morning long, the oars of the rowboats moving among the fishing boats from the breaks to the docks make joyful sounds as they are pulled in and out of the calm waters. The oars cut into the water, then out, then in, then out, then in....

A park stretches in front of the station; this was the park I played in as a child. I am thinking about the playgrounds, patrolled by the colorful dreams of wealthy neighborhoods, which once upon a time appeared so colorful to me. Now as the wind blows, the sharp odor of rust coming off the swings and slide meets my nostrils with a cold slap. One of the chains of the swing I played on when I was seven has snapped off and the seat hangs down in tired dejection. I think about how much I must have weighed then. The chain is determined to swing in the face of the strong wind. It must have been this stubbornness that makes the thin layer of rust on its surface look like weathered leather as the sun beats full upon it.

A pool of water has formed under the swing. I shiver in fear. For a moment, the shallow hole holding the water becomes a bottomless pit sucking me in. Then just as my breathing begins to fail and I am engulfed by overriding panic, I find myself swinging up, up towards the sky again. And then the downward dip again. Overcome by the horrifying thought of disappearing into the depths of the pit, I say, "This is the last time." I am stubbornly clenching my hands in tight fists, my fingernails biting deep into the palms of my hands.

"This is the last time. This is the last time. This is the last time."

I'm at the top of Balipaşa Hill, the steep road that runs straight down the hill. My eyes are locked onto the sea. And then I let myself go, my body bolting downwards. I am clutching a kite in one hand, and as I run down the hill, I feel that my feet will leave the pavement before I get to the end of the road. And they do. I'm in the air now, that fear of the end again engulfing me: "This is the last time." As soon as I think this, the fear evaporates. And again. This time I won't make it. I am flying one way and then the other in a crazy fit, like a balloon, its air slowly being let out.

I find myself in front of my father's heating stove shop. I open my fist and set the kite free, letting it fly away into the sky.

It was a long run and I'm out of breath. I enter the shop in a state of panic. The door shuts of its own accord.

The windows cloud up. My father is across the street at Bekir's coffeehouse, playing cards with his friends. He keeps one eye on the shop as he plays, so he knows that I have come. His body is completely relaxed and his sense of well-being has erased any lines from his face. My father is forty years old.

I feel strange somehow when I first enter his shop. I close my eyes tightly so as to better inhale the smells of this place. The recognition of these smells obliterates any strangeness I had felt. There's a smell of tin and then of the sharp odor of enamel paint that tugs at my nostrils. And then there is the heavy smell of the grease my father uses on the gears. I open my eyes. Everything I see now smiles as if to say, "Welcome." The glass in the window embraces my warm breath and holds it there. It's cold outside. People are hurrying down the Balipaşa Hill to get to the station as fast as they possibly can.

My eyes travel over the wooden top counter and the tools

44

hanging from nails above the worktable. My father has moved the clock with its cracked face. The clock was always hung next to the monkey wrenches, but now it hangs next to the smallest of his adjustment pliers. The hand of the clock points at a spot just below the crack. Seven o'clock. There are still two hours till closing. Even though it gets dark earlier in winter, my father keeps the shop open later because winter is the season to sell heating stoves. People on their way home from work in the evening may stop by to purchase a stove, if they hadn't bought one yet that season, or some needed stovepipes.

The door opens and a man steps into the shop. He's a big man and he's wearing a kind of plaid jacket. The man's large body seems to fill every space in the tiny shop. As if that isn't enough, the coldness from outside enters as well, making the room icy cold again, just as the shop had begun to warm up. The man rubs his hands together to warm himself.

Because of my short hair, it does not even occur to the man that I might be a girl.

"Son, how much are those narrow tin pipes?"

It's easier for me to make out the features of his face now that he is talking. His mustache, trimmed to a half centimeter above his lip seems to be an indication of his stinginess.

"A hundred and twenty-five liras."

I can see his muscles tighten as he straightens up sternly before me. His face sulks suddenly in an expression of his discomfort at having to be dealing with a child.

"How can that be? It's not gold after all; it's just a piece of tin. The government should be controlling these prices! Everybody is free to charge as much as they want! So, how much are the enamel ones then?"

45

"There are no narrow enamel pipes left. We only have the wide ones. And they cost three hundred and twenty-five liras."

"Son, call your father or your boss or whoever it is who is in charge of this store!"

"Even if my father comes, the price will stay the same!"

The answer seems to echo from the many years that have passed since it was spoken and helps me to come to myself. The door of the store I see reflected in the pool of water gradually takes on the shape of my face. I slowly edge back to reality. I am repeating to myself, over and over:

"Even if my father comes, the price will stay the same!"

I become unable to touch others. My voice cannot be heard. Everything and everyone is moving and nobody, nobody notices me. I look to the sky. The tail of my kite is just about to disappear from view. I regret having set it free. The loud and disorderly noise of turning wheels blocks out the voices of people and the sounds emanating from work places and turns my being upside-down. I hide behind a door. It is not much later that I find myself wandering about the streets.

I am at the end of the Gedikpaşa Hill road and I am looking at Aunt Sabiha's house, a house with its face turned towards the main street. A huge truck is barreling down the hill. Its brakes have burst. Aunt Sabiha, seeing the now rabid truck heading straight for her front door, throws the laundry she has been hanging into the air in a fit of panic and screams at the top of her lungs.

"Quick! Neighbors, come quickly! My house is coming down! Neighbors!"

The truck swallows up Aunt Sabiha's screams and with all its might smashes into the heavy wooden doors of the house. At that moment, the truck looked like a small fish, half of its body twitching in final fits of discomfiture in the mouth of a big fish that had just half-swallowed it. Helplessness. Or like the sorrowful end of a stillborn tortoise pup, half of its body hanging out of the mother's body, her cries devastating the peacefulness of the sea. Aunt Sabiha's voice pummels through time, picking up speed like the swiftness of an arrow.

My mother's voice is calling me home. And just like always, she calls at the most exciting part of the game, just when I have really gotten into it. We're playing burning ball. The cars are speeding past us. Just like a ball. I run in circles, turning this way and that to avoid the ball being aimed at me. I am moving up and down the street again and again. As I speed up, so does the blood pumping through my veins. The faster I go, the more I sweat. I think that the faster I move, the sooner coolness will be mine.

At about eight-thirty or so, it's time for my father to come home. He suddenly comes into view as he rounds the corner. He's wearing his green jacket and he's getting his key ready to unlock the door. He looks cold like always and is quickening his steps, anxious to get home. And just as he steps over the threshold he says the same thing that he says on every winter's day.

"*Vay, vay, vay*, I have never in my life seen such a cold winter's day."

I grab unto his jacket before he has had the chance to shut the door.

"*Baba*, won't you give me some money?"

I envision each of the colorfully wrapped pieces of candy displayed in the window of Uncle Bedros' grocery store. My father hesitates. He cannot withstand the pleading look in my eyes, so reaches into his pocket. The roof of my mouth can already taste the sweet pink confection.

"Nope, no money."

"Not even two liras? Please! *Baba*!"

"Nope, no change."

The taste of the candy does not reach the ice cream cone, but is left frozen on the roof of my mouth as the door is shut in my face.

Someone is pulling me onto the sidewalk. A dark blue car quickly passes me by. The dark blue slowly becomes the blue of a road that leads me to the entrance of my elementary school with its gray paint. I walk through the dark blue of the door into the gray world that lies beyond it. Sounds are coming from the classrooms. Soon there are children everywhere. One of them is thin, with tight, curly hair and knock-kneed legs. This is the type of child who consistently prods those to her right and left and just can't seem to stand still. This is me. Me, after all these years. This is me. How exciting! I move over to stand across from myself.

"Hi there! I'm you!"

Little Me looks up at me with wide open eyes. Her pupils are as large and foggy as they can possibly be, on the verge of turning into a rain of tears. I'm sorry as I think that I have frightened Little Me. I open my arms to Little Me, preparing to embrace her with my entire body. But she glides right through my body and runs to my mother who is standing directly behind me. My mother looks at me, her eyes inquiring as to what has happened. All of a sudden, Little Me breaks into tears.

"I don't know. I don't know."

Actually, I know what happened that day. And so does Little

Me. We walk together into the office of the vice-principal, who is also our Turkish teacher. The vice-principal tells me to sit down and then begins to talk to my mother. Although that strident tone he uses with students has softened into a honeyed flow when talking to my mother, the expression in his eyes stills reflects the state of a tamed predatory bird.

"Actually, she's one of the best readers in the class, but today something happened to her and I don't understand why. She couldn't read the topic I gave in class today. And she still couldn't read it, even when I scolded her. I am sorry to have to tell you this, but I think there's something wrong with her eyes." The tired expression in my mother's eyes that reflects how foreign she feels to what's happening around her takes on an air of hopelessness as she listens to the vice-principal. Her body seems to grow smaller in the chair in which she sits. For an instant, her gaze fixes upon her daughter's wide-open pupils. While the vice-principal is telling my mother to get me to an eye doctor, my mother's small body, which seemed to be getting smaller and smaller, suddenly comes to and redefines itself across from the vice-principal. Her cheeks flush and the crease between her eyes grows deeper. With an angry expression, she turns to Little Me who has tried to take advantage of the teacher's good intentions. She shakes her head back and forth as if to say, "You've made me a partner to this deception, too!" I realize then that my mother looks angry enough to pluck out Little Me's eyes. She swallows hard before turning to the vice-principal.

"The other day I took her older brother to an ophthalmologist and he gave us some drops to dilate the pupils. I would guess that she put some of those drops into her eyes."

49

The vice-principal looks sternly at Little Me.

"How many drops did you use?" he asks.

Little Me answers, tears streaming down my face with such force I might shed my pupils themselves as well.

"I didn't want to..."

My mother interrupts.

"You didn't want to! You didn't want to! As if I didn't know you! Tell us, how many drops?"

Little Me sniffles, "Four. My brother put in two and I put in two more."

My mother leaves Little Me just like that at school. Her silence is a good indication of the scolding Little Me is to get later at home.

It's our street again. It draws me to it like a magnet. And my mother's voice again, "I told you to get into the house right now!" I reluctantly go into the house and head straight for the toilet. As soon as my mother opens the bathroom door, she sees what's happened. The warm liquid is running down my legs and turning to steam in the cold cubicle.

"My God, girl, did you pee standing up again? The Good Lord knows what I have suffered because of you!"

Little Me looks quite funny as she holds onto the five inch plastic hose. I burst out laughing. Even looking like this she still manages to get her words in.

"If you don't tell my Baba to buy me a *çuk*, I'm going to use this hose to pee standing up every day."

My mother is trying to control her anger as she pleads,

"Listen Honey, you're a girl. Girls don't have *çuk*s to begin with. And they never get one put on later."

Little Me's eyes become open faucets.

"Do you mean I'll never have a *çuk*?"

The next day Big Me is there when my mother comes to school.

I keep trying to show myself to my mother. I shout.

"Quick, take Little Me home. Gramma hasn't died yet."

If my mother hadn't met the principal at the door and gone into her room to talk, I could have seen my grandmother one last time. But I couldn't make my voice heard. Little Me bombards my mother with incessant questions.

"Why did you come? Where are you taking me?"

Little Me finally stops asking when mother tells the principal that I have a cold and she wants to take me to the doctor. I'm still trying to make myself heard, however, so we can hurry and go home. The more I try, the more energy I expend. I keep running back and forth and shouting as loud as I can to make myself heard, but it is all to no avail.

My eyes mist over and then the rivers begin to flow. The more the tears flow, the thicker becomes the glass wall that divides us. The children, my mother, Little Me, and everything else stay on the other side of the glass. The gray color that predominates around us gives way to air the color of ice. The activity on the other side of the glass first slows down and then the sounds grow more and more distant. The glass grows even thicker as more tears flow from my eyes. The view on the other side is enveloped in a deep and icy mass before it disappears altogether.

The girl from Kastamonu calls to me. She throws down five liras and asks me to buy her a picture novel. She calls after me, "The latest issue." I run down Gedikpaşa Hill Road with all my might. Bedri's grocery is at the bottom of the hill. The grocer

Bedri is a Tartar with almond-shaped eyes. His face is sullen as always. While straightening up the magazines on the shelf, he asks me what I want, even though he knows the answer. I tell him I want a "picture novel - the latest issue!" Just as swiftly as I snatch the slim book from his hands, I plop down my money and dash out of the shop. When I get to their house, the Kastamonu girl shouts down that the door is open. I find her waiting for me at the top of the stairs. She takes the picture novel from my hand and presses an apple into its place. On my way out she reminds me to shut the door tight. I sit on the sidewalk on the other side of the street. While eating my apple I look up. The only thing I see is her elbow sticking out of the window frame.

I throw the apple stem high into the air; it spins around some and then falls slowly to the ground. A piece of metal spins around in a whirl of imbalance. Then it stops. It's a gold ring with green stones staring up at me. The shininess of the stones dazzles my eyes. The children crowd around me. As I bend over to pick up the ring without letting the others see what I am doing, the now dirt-covered apple core rubs against my hand.

I wipe my dirty hand on my jeans, surrounded by a chorus of children begging me to tell them a story.

"A man lost a ring that he had inherited from his ancestors and a whole generation later the ring was found by one of his great-grandchildren. And the child found it without going to any trouble whatsoever. It sounds strange but the ring just showed up one day in front of her. Yes, that's right. While she was walking along, what should she see in the dirt but the ring that had belonged to the grandfather of the grandfather of her grand-father."

This was the first story I ever told. Or at least one of the first stories I ever told. The children all listen to me with their mouths wide open. Even though Medine is always on the point of objecting, I can quiet her with a quick look of my eyes. She knows full well that compliance is her only way out. After a while, it becomes utterly unimportant that the legend is actually a lived event. The children believe that I have been awarded for knowing the events of such a story and so they slowly distance themselves from the legend and look at me in awe.

A window of the house across the street opens and an old woman sticks her head out, "What are you children doing ganging up down there? All you kids with no manners!"

With one voice we drown out her shouts: "Police Lady! Police Lady!"

She is the police lady. Her dead husband had been a policeman and her oldest son is a retired police officer. Her dead husband's medals hang from pins on the chest of her dress. The ribbons on the medals have left stains on her dress fronts.

"Get out of here, you little bitches! Get away now or I'll call the police!"

The Police Lady flings two full jars of water down into the street and we all scatter like baby chicks. The sharp points of the glass shards shine up to the sky. The large pieces of glass overturn and rock back and forth for a while like turtles on their backs. Aunt Ayşe appears at her door with a bucket of water that she throws into the street to wash away the broken glass. She dumps out the water with all her might so that the water will drive the glass away. The water laps up the glass, the tiny pieces of glass turning somersaults in the rivulets as they take on shape and color and roll down the street.

Cevat starts shouting, "A head span! A head span!"

He measures the distance he has hit the marble with another by spans. It is exactly the span of his head. No more. No less.

"We won! We won!"

We always beat the other kids at marbles. When I play marbles with anyone other than Cevat, I always lose. The same is true for Cevat. He has to play with me to win. When I get home with my pockets and undershirt stuffed with marbles, my mother pours them in a pot and then takes them out to the garden with me on her heels, my snotty nose running full speed. In the front part of our garden there's a foundation hole about thirty feet deep. She dumps my marbles down the hole while I hold my breath.

The marbles absorb the rays of the sun and before my eyes they begin to turn and turn with their colors melting into one another until they fall onto the soil. They spread out all over the ground. Suddenly, I become rooted in my very place. The two marbles of my eyes are turned to the heavens. The sky becomes hazy streaks of green, blue, orange, red, and purple. I am breathing deeply. I inhale each of the buildings and begin to dance amidst the colors.

I awake filled with dread at the sound that the train, coming full speed down the tracks, emits as it becomes one with the wind. That sound is drowned out by the honking of the horns of cars travelling down the shore road and by the noise made when the street people with snarls and curses smash their empty bottles of cheap Marmara wine against the old city walls, as if to curse their fates. My search for shelter ends in the naked park dotted with disembodied stumps of trees. As I run my eyes over the rusty metal, I realize that the single chain that had been holding up the swing has come off as well.

STATION TRILOGY II

THE DİYARBAKIR - İSTANBUL LINE

Ever since the train pulled out of the station at Diyarbakır, the overriding heat has been fading, ever so slowly, as if this were a trip straight into coolness. The passengers who boarded the train in the 40-degree heat of Diyarbakır's simmering August weather have finally begun to free themselves of the feeling that they will be carrying that same heat with them all the way to Istanbul. A woman is sitting next to the window with a young five or six year old child on her lap. The child has melted against her mother's body like limp dough. Her half-closed eyes only partially open when the train makes a sudden movement but then soon regain their earlier heaviness. Her head rests against her mother's breast where the child is rocked to the beating of her mother's heart, "tick, tick, tick...." while her other ear is soothed by the takir-tikir of the train moving along the tracks. The two sounds have become a rhythm reverberating through her brain: tick-tick-tick, takir-tikir. She falls asleep.

Next to them sits Fahriye with her three children, across from them Hazal with her four. As the hours progress, the children begin to shake off the unfamiliarity of the compartmental surroundings. One of them -nine year-old Musto- takes charge and suggests a round of singing.

When the child sitting in her mother's lap hears this suggestion, her eyes open wide and in no time she dives into the midst of the others. The children's voices rise in a shouting match, each crying "Me first, me first, me first," until Musto finds a solution to put an end to the chaos. Pushing and pulling, he makes the children form a line. "Now I'm going to count. Whoever I'm pointing at in the end will go first."

"Our earth is round,

but our moonlight abounds.

All we need is milk and bread,

show to me the color red."

He says one syllable of the rhyme for each child, sometimes elongating the sounds so as to make sure the last syllable lands on himself. All the while, the children are busy concentrating on the swiftly moving index finger. Finally, Musto comes to the last syllable, which he draws out, skipping over four of the other children and thus succeeding in his mission to be the first to sing, which he loses no time in doing.

He starts with the children's school pledge: *"Türküm, doğruyum, çalışkanım. Yasam, küçüklerimi korumak, büyüklerimi saymak..."*(I'm a Turk, I'm honest, I'm industrious. I pledge to protect those younger than myself and to respect my elders.) He makes the pledge in Turkish, deeply accented by his native Kurdish.

He repeats the pledge in a singsong voice at least five or six times. Hazal praises her son, "Good for you, Musto. Sing, sing and keep the rest quiet."

The children leave the compartment and join up with the other children on the train, their loud voices in the corridor multiplying along with their numbers. The women begin to converse among themselves. They talk about the trials and tribulations of just getting by these days, using the price per pound of the cucumber Hazal is peeling as a springboard for discussion. Fahriye says that her situation isn't much different from Hazal's. In her language — a mixture of Turkish and Kurdish — she tells them, "The kids, they eat and eat but never seem to get filled up. Well, let them eat and let them grow and then, Allah willing, they will grow up and they will feed us. 'Course, only Allah knows if they will or not..."

Every now and then she glances at the woman sitting in the corner looking out the window. She tries to draw her into the conversation, but the woman is not even aware that there has been an invitation to talk. She has left her sick mother in Diyarbakır and is now on her way back to Istanbul. The pain of this separation and her mother's illness seems to sharpen with each kilometer that comes between them.

Hazal's patience has run out and her curiosity taken over:

"Do you live in Istanbul, *Bacı*?"

"Yes, I do. My mother lives in Diyarbakır. She's ill so I came to visit her."

"Where do you live in Istanbul?"

"In Kumkapı."

Hazal's eyes begin to sparkle. She knows nothing about Istanbul, but this woman has named the place her husband had told her about.

"Us too; us too," she says with great excitement. "Well, actually, we are just going to Istanbul for the first time. My man and Fahriye's here, well, they're business partners. And that place you just said, that's where they rented a place for us. They say the house is nice, but the only thing is that it's full of *cirdon*. But that's okay!"

Fahriye is quick to intercede, "What's to be afraid of *cirdon*? We'll set some traps and that'll be the end of them. " Her face beams with happiness at the insignificance of the problem.

"What traps?" asked Hazal. "We'll just sic these seven kids on 'em and watch how fast they get out!"

She turns to Fahriye, "Hey, what's the name of that place they work?"

"In the name of Allah, what was it then? Oh yeah, it's something with a "paşa.""

The woman at the window is quick to identify the place, "Mahmutpaşa," she says. Now she can't suppress her own curiosity. "Do they have a store there?"

Hazal begins to explain with words full of the excitement and pride she feels for their venture. "Well, *Abla*, Allah be praised, in one sense, it's a big job. They display their goods on the ground. They sell clothes and stuff like that. Now, just between the two of us, well, actually, you're a sister to us now, so we can talk about this between us, what they do is kind of secret.... I mean, the city doesn't really know about it. Everyday the city inspectors come and chase them off. Then our men move around from street to street for a while until they come back to the same place and open up their packs again. One of these inspectors was *kirve* for one of the boys on Fahriye's husband's side of the family."

Fahriye interrupts Hazal, "*He, hee*, that was Reşid of the Silo family."

Hazal continues, "He told them that when the city gets tired of chasing them, they'll leave 'em alone. The thing is to not give up."

As she talks, her eyebrows appear to move together and her face takes on the stern expression of her husband as she repeats his words.

"My man says that the city in that Paşa place should just give us a place on the ground to work and every three months I'll put up a good building in the very center of Istanbul."

Fahriye seconds what Hazal has to say by nodding her head continuously and adding her "*he-hee*'s."

Hazal finishes what she has to say in no time. Both women now look towards the third woman, waiting to hear her tell her story. The woman, though, seems to have neither the inclination nor the determination to relate anything of her own life. She thinks to herself, "Maybe I was like these two, too, on my first trip to Istanbul." Just then, her child comes back into the compartment and again curls into her lap. While continuing with her "*he-hee*'s", Fahriye turns to the child sitting in her mother's lap.

"Our children are all playing together out there. I pray to Allah that they will all grow into great people for His sake."

She again looks at the woman.

"*Abla*, is your child sick?"

The woman straightens up. She is perspiring heavily.

"No, why would you think so? She's fine, thanks be to God."

"It's just that, *Abla*, our children are casting around like a ringing church bell. This heat doesn't affect 'em one way or another. Just let her go with them and see how she acts!"

The woman shakes her head.

"Don't think that she's always like this. She's no quieter than any of the rest."

Suddenly one of the children runs into the compartment and shouts as loud as he can: "*Daye*, the man has got Musto; he's hitting him!"

Hazal puts down the paper sack of cucumbers she's been holding and puts her hands on her waist.

"As Allah is my witness, Ömer, what 'man' and where and why is he hitting Musto?"

Ömer tears his olive black eyes from his mother and runs back into the corridor so as not to miss a second of the beating his brother Musto is getting. His mother stands up as though this were an entirely familiar situation. She smooths her long, cotton, floral print dress into order and reties her head covering under her chin before going out into the corridor. She reenters almost before she has had the chance to leave. The conductor has Musto by the arm and is dragging him along, forcing him into the compartment. The compartment now seems filled with the crowd of children and the screaming and yelling, and it's almost impossible to breathe. Because he works the Diyarbakır-Istanbul line, the conductor speaks a strange Turkish, basically the heavy eastern accent of Diyarbakır that he has tried to soften with a stylized and overly-refined version of Istanbul Turkish. He's short and thin, but the glare of his eyes tells one and all not to be fooled by his size. He turns to stare into the eyes of his prisoner - Musto - and begins the inquisition.

"Whose child is this?"

"He's mine. Whatever he has done you have the loan of my neck to break his bones with. It is truth to Allah, sir, that the heat has gone to their heads and they have all have gone rabid. You scold them, because, Allah knows, they won't listen to me!"

Hazal towers over the conductor both in weight and height and it is obvious from the rapidity of her speech that this is a ploy she is well accustomed to using. She stands facing the man, trying with all her might not to break into laughter. Hazal's all too easy bestowal of her son prevents the conductor from venting his anger, so he starts to expand on the crime, transforming it into a national grievance.

"You see what he's like today. Kids like this, ones who don't listen, they grow up to be anarchists. Today they are my problems, but tomorrow they will be the nation's problems."

Hazal keeps nodding her head in assent to the conductor's words. This signification of approval is not only for the words currently coming out of the conductor's mouth, but also pre-approval for the words to follow. However, the conductor's last remarks bring her up short and she stops nodding her head, feeling the need now to insert her own remarks.

"Allah forbid! Allah forbid! Our family doesn't get involved in anything like that. My children are going to go to school and make something of themselves. My man says..."

She pauses for a second as she registers the fact that Musto's face still reflects indifference despite his ear being held hostage by the conductor who is pulling it up tightly at an angle. She continues, "Listen you, Musto, do you hear me? When we get to Istanbul, I am going to tell your father what you have been up to! And you know what he will do!"

His brothers and sisters begin to poke and pinch each other with laughter as they hear their mother scold their older brother, and they begin shouting in unison, "*Baba*'s going to beat his butt. *Baba*'s going to beat Musto's butt!"

Musto is now looking around for anyone in the group who will back him up while he struggles to break free of the conductor's hold. After the seven children have their fill of loudly teasing Musto, they choose one last taunt to bring him to his knees.

"Butt raw Musto! Butt raw Musto!"

The conductor releases Musto's ear, a look of panic on his face. He just wants to get out of this compartment as quickly as possible. He points his finger at Hazal.

"Lady, you can beat his behind all you want. That's up to you. But hear me now. If I find this little bastard peeing on the compartment doors one more time during this trip, let me tell you now that I'll cut his *çuk* right off of him!"

Musto is now hiding behind his mother's skirts. Without even realizing it, his hand has gone to the front of his trousers, where he unzips his zipper, and with great fear tightly clasps his treasure.

When the conductor leaves the compartment Hazal is still pinching and prodding Musto and pulling him out in front of her. Musto knows full well what is in store for him now, so he puts all his faith in the soles of his shoes and shoots out into the corridor in search of a good hiding place. The rest of the children run out behind him.

Hazal stops speaking and turns to the woman sitting opposite from her.

"City kids act a whole lot different," she says.

The woman is quick to reply that city kids aren't always as obedient as they may look.

Fahriye has her own take on the issue.

"Our kids are Allah's wrath upon us. May Allah forbid that yours become problems for you."

The woman did not feel the need to reply to this point. Just then, having thought of something funny, Hazal suddenly bursts into loud laughter. Only she knows what she is laughing about.

When she finally gets control of herself, she asks the others, "Did you see that guy?"

Fahriye joins in, "And don't you wonder what his wife looks like?"

She had touched upon just the subject Hazal was longing to bring up. Leaning forward in her seat, Hazal draws the two other women closer to her. She is blushing.

When she can finally stop laughing again long enough to talk she manages to sputter, "If his wife is bigger than he is, who do you suppose goes on top?" Both of her listeners laugh, while checking the door to make sure no one is listening in on this conversation. Their faces reflect the shameful joy one feels at exploring someone else's bedroom.

The morning is thus spent before the train pulls into the first station along the way. The child is again nestling in her mother's arms half-asleep. This time sleep isn't brought on by the heat and the rhythm of the tracks but rather by the exhaustion of running through the train with the pack of children. When the train pulls out again, the sun is at its highest point, leaving needles of light to pierce the windows of the compartment. The tracks are smoother now and the takir-tiker noise has disappeared.

The compartment with its eight children is slowly coming to life. At noon, a piece of unleavened bread is pressed into each child's hand as the children get ready to again explore every possible nook and cranny of the train. The door to their compartment is standing open. A large-built man suddenly bursts through the door of the neighboring compartment and noises suddenly begin to echo along the corridor.

"Cumalı, please, I kiss your hands and your feet, please

don't hit me."

"But it was all right for you when you were making eyes at the bastard, wasn't it? You come here and kiss the horns you're putting on my head!"

"I don't even know the man. Stop hitting me. You're making a horrible scene!"

"You should have thought of that before you started making eyes at the lousy *kıbrağ.*

"Cumalı, please stop. I'll lick the fat of your eyes, but please stop. For the sake of our poor eight kids, stop."

The shouts continue until the conductor hears what is happening and intercedes. As he leaves the compartment, he can be heard muttering to himself, "This nation of women has all turned into anarchists. How are we ever going to get the better of them?"

He strikes with all his might at one of the children who happens to cross his path. While the others take off running to the safety of their mothers, the victim of the beating, Musto, is running away, ahead of the conductor.

When everything finally settles down, monotony once again descends upon the train and its passengers. Seven children decide at the same time that they have to pee this very instant, so the two mothers set off with their children in tow for a trip to the train toilet. The neighboring compartment door is open and Cumali is standing at the corridor window as he smokes a cigarette. The rays of the sun strike against the gold of his wristwatch. Seeing him, the women quickly pull the lower parts of their muslin head coverings over their mouths and, averting their eyes, quickly pass by. In the process, each woman can't help but take a good look at Cumali out of the corner of her eye. Just five steps later both women break into giggles. Hazal hits Ömer on the top of his head to drown out the sounds of their laughter.

"Hey you there, hold your pee. You just better not pee in your pants!"

Cumali tosses his cigarette butt out of the window. With a politeness of voice unexpected from a man who just ten minutes earlier had been beating his wife, he turns to the Istanbul woman sitting inside the compartment and says, "*Abla*, I can close this window if it's disturbing you."

The child opens her eyes wide, staring with undisguised fear at this big man with his loud and heavy voice. When his eyes meet those of the child, he approaches them where they are sitting. The child buries herself as deeply as she possibly can into her mother's lap as if she is trying to disappear from view. The man begins to stroke the child's head as he turns to speak to the woman.

"*Abla*, who do you have in Istanbul?"

"We live in Istanbul. I came to Diyarbakır to visit my mother."

The man appears to have satisfied his curiosity and continues to stroke the child's head. The child's fear has not yet dissipated. As he strokes the child's head he softly says, "*Kürdo, Kürdo.*" The child raises her head and looks at the man with wide eyes.

"I'm not Kurdish. I'm Armenian."

The woman becomes fearful of the man's reactions to this disclosure and pinches her child on her rear end to warn her not to speak further. These words which have so naturally poured out of the child's mouth are embraced by hearty laughter coming straight from the man's heart. The laugh seems to spread in broad waves from his dark face and through his body where it mixes and mingles with the sounds of the train itself. He turns on his heels and walks out of the compartment, shaking his head from side to side.

The child is still surprised at the pain of the pinch and asks her mother with deep curiosity.

"Mama, what's a Kurd and what's an Armenian?"

Hazal and Fahriye reenter the compartment with Musto in tow. Hazal, carrying two pairs of wet underpants, tries to stuff the underpants into a corner of the suitcase which has been tied close with a thick rope because of its broken zipper. Musto pulls at his mother's skirt.

"*Daye, Daye*, why did you say the man had horns? What does it mean for a man to have horns?" His mother answers with a quick and heavy blow to his back with her fist. The women send each other quizzical looks.

"Aren't you ashamed of yourself for listening in on woman's talk?"

When she raises her fist to hit him again, Musto takes off running out of the compartment. The rhythm of his plastic shoes hitting the corridor floor beats in time with the rhythm of his shouts, "Horned *kıbrağ*. Horned *kıbrağ*."

It's around eleven thirty at night when the train pulls into another station. The sky is awash with stars, lighting up the station at night. A sweet chorus of crickets living in the bushes along the tracks serenade the stars with a soft lullaby. No one gets off the train but two new passengers hurriedly board. The train then sets off to travel through a light tunnel of stars before disappearing into the night. Just an hour later, the train comes to a sudden halt. In vain the passengers peer out of the darkness of their windows to see a station. Those who were sleeping now awake as speculations spread from car to car and compartment to compartment. "Someone has blocked the way." "The train has hit a cow." "A rail is missing." "Some bastard has fallen under the train."

The loudspeaker begins to issue commands. "Everyone must stay aboard. No one is to disembark from the train."

This is followed by a second announcement, delivered in the voice of the conductor. "Parents, take control of your children. We are not responsible if a child gets lost. If any child stays here, we will not come back to pick him up!"

Even though his tone of voice is not quite as effective as that of a military commander, it is still quite threatening and this leads to the spreading of even more frightening stories.

Other than those who are too young to comprehend what's going on, all members of the eight-child compartment wait in dreadful unease, their fear intensifying by the moment. The same is true for most of the rest of the compartments.

Hazal's youngest daughter Neriman announces that she has to pee. This time the three women set out with their eight children in tow for a toilet tour. They have a hard time making their way down the corridor as passengers have lined up at the corridor windows and are trying to see something in the darkness outside. When they finally make it to the toilets, they find a long line in front of them. A strong odor issues from the toilets. The women cover their mouths with their headscarves to filter out the noxious fumes. Every now and then, they uncover their mouths long enough to exhale with disgust and make a whole range of grimaces as they curse the smell. The children enter the toilet in ones and twos while the women talk among themselves. The more they talk, the more far out their speculations become. A woman with five or six inches of gold bangles on each of her forearms attracts great attention as she claims to have been an eyewitness to the events.

"I just couldn't sleep so I was staring out the window. And suddenly I saw a man fall off the train."

As the gold-braided bangles begin to weigh onto the woven reed bracelet she wears closest to her wrist, she pulls down the sleeve of her dress as if to conceal the bracelets. This, of course, attracts even more attention to her person.

One of the women asks, "How did he fall?"

"Well, *Abla*, let me tell you this much. I saw a light behind him. It shone so brightly into my eyes that I couldn't even see my hand... you might say I was blinded."

This makes the crowd of women even more frightened, and it is soon the common belief that the accident could only be the work of a supernatural force.

"It was a djinn!" shouts a woman, "*Allahumma enni auzubke mınal habsı vel habais*, hoping that this prayer will protect her from the power of these evil forces.

This news spreads so quickly that the voices of the women rise and blend with a kind of shrill scream. Much of the keening sound is coming from Cumali's wife who is crying as she beats her knees.

"The train hadn't stopped yet when Cumali got up to go to the toilet. That's the last I saw of him. He must have jumped off the train. Oh my God, what's to become of us and what's to become of my poor, orphaned children?"

The knot of women is now intent on consoling Cumali's wife. The woman with the bracelets is still trying to tell and retell her tale and realizes that the attention has now turned to another direction. She breaks off her story and in a pretentious tone starts to comfort Cumali's wife, "No, *Abla*, no. Why think of bad things. Maybe it wasn't him."

"It was him. I know it. I know it. He's nowhere to be found. My cooking fire has gone out!" So saying, the woman turns around and takes her clinging and crying children with her back to their compartment.

One woman has had enough of the whole situation and blurts out, "Yeah, right, first she puts horns on her husband and then he throws himself off the train just to get rid of his shame! The whore! Now she beats her knees!"

All the women agree and begin to praise the one among them who has the courage to actually say what they had all been thinking. While Fahriye is cleaning her five year-old daughter's bottom with a pair of dirty underwear she also manages to squeeze in a few comments of her own.

"That woman's djinn pushed her husband out of the train."

The line in front of the toilet has grown into a gossip factory. The speculations arise here, are kneaded and given form, and then quickly distributed throughout the train.

The conductor's voice is heard before he comes into view.

"Okay, ladies, break it up now. Haven't your kids finished their peeing yet? That's enough. Get back to your husbands now. This is not the time for talking. Everybody is to go back to their own seats immediately! This is not the time for peeing..."

One of the women quickly covers her mouth with her scarf and immediately lowers her eyes to the floor.

"What can we do, Sir? They're just children and can't hold their pee."

The conductor raises his eyebrows and gives a disinterested retort. "You should teach them to hold it."

He is well aware of the hate-filled stares delivered in his direction. As the women are sent back to their seats, he can hear one of them declare, "It should have been the conductor who was pushed off the train!"

His retort is hard on her heels. "I hope to Allah that when you die you sit up straight in your *gor.*'

When they get back to the compartment, Fahriye realizes that she is still carrying the dirty pair of underpants. "I'll see you in your grave," she yells at her daughter as she pulls up her trousers.

The train is in a state of excited expectation. Most of the children have drifted off to sleep while the women chew over and over again the events of the night until they have explored all possibilities and now wait in silence for the eventual outcome. The child with her head on her mother's lap opens one eye and tells her mother she has to pee. The woman stands up and takes her daughter by the hand and out into the corridor but the young girl is still half-asleep. When the child looks up imploringly into her mother's eyes, she glances down and understands the problem. The urine dripping down the young girl's legs is forming a pool.

"God damn it. This was all I needed! For God's sakes, girl, why did you get up to pee if you were just gonna do it on the floor?"

When they get back to the compartment, the two women greet them with inquisitive looks.

"She wet herself before I even got her to the toilet."

Fahriye is quick to add, "She's a child, *Abla*, of course she's gonna pee. If you could only see what my kids do..."

The woman is concerned. "Yes, I know, but this is her last pair of underpants."

Despite her large body, Hazal is up like a flash. She unties her suitcase and begins rummaging through it until she pulls out a pair of underpants that she hands to the woman.

"Here, *Abla*, take these."

The woman looks at the underpants with their large, dried urine stain and says, "That's all right. I'll manage."

Using both hands, Hazal tries to show her that the underpants have dried. Suddenly the conductor's voice is heard over the loudspeakers.

"The train has stopped here due to a minor mechanical problem. The problem has been fixed. The train will depart in five minutes time. Despite what's being said, absolutely no one has fallen off the train. This is just a bunch of worthless talk. The passenger who supposedly fell off has been seen coming out of his compartment."

Hazal and Fahriye look at each other with great surprise. They seem almost sorry that no one has fallen off the train.

"It was all started by that lousy bitch, that daughter of a whore!" mutters Hazal with irritation at this turn of events.

Musto is back in the corridor when the train takes off. His plastic shoes beat along the corridor with a rhythm matched by the growly voice emitting from his throat.

"Daughter of a whore, lousy bitch; daughter of a whore, lousy bitch."

STATION TRILOGY III

SİRKECİ - HALKALI LINE

The train has just pulled out of the Kazlıçeşme Station. Two teenage boys of around 16 or 17 are talking loudly in the middle of the crowded car.

"How many mussels did you sell?"

"Thirty-two."

"How much money did you get?"

"Eight hundred thousand."

"How many you got left?"

"Sixty-eight."

"Did you lose any shells?"

"Three fell on the ground in Sirkeci. Everybody was looking at me, so I kicked "em under the tracks."

"Now you've eaten shit! You'll have to go to the *meyhane* tomorrow and find some shells."

"No, I can't. They'll be too big. Ma's gonna get mad "cuz they'll take too much rice."

Just at that point a voice calls out of the crowd

"Mussel man!"

"I'm here, *Abi*."

"How much?"

"Twenty-five thousand."

The man takes a hundred thousand lira bill out of his pocket.

"Give me four, four of the big ones."

"Of course, *Abi*."

The mussel seller expertly opens four of the closed mussels. In the most mouth-watering and theatrical manner possible, he squirts each with lemon juice, holding the lemon high above the mussels to gain the best possible effect. He places the top shell under the rice stuffing like a spoon and lines the four mussels up on his rack for the customer to eat. As soon as the man eats the first, he tosses the empty shell out of the train window. The other passengers in the car look at him with undisguised distain, but no one says anything. The mussel seller waits in vain for someone in the crowd to raise a fuss. After finishing the four mussels and after throwing all of their shells out of the train window, the man takes out another hundred thousand lira bill and asks for another four.

"With a lot of lemon juice!"

"Coming right up, *Abi*!"

While the mussel seller is deep in thought, wondering what to do about his mussel shells, another child begins pulling on the sleeve of his brother who is selling *simit*.

"Abi, how much is a *simit*?"

"How much you got?"

"Fifteen thousand!"

"It's not enough but... I'll make an exception in your case," he says as he chooses one of the stale simits he had placed among the fresh. "Here you go, I'll give you a cheap one just this very one time."

73

With a grateful expression the child bites happily into his *simit*.

As the train pulls into the Yenikapı station, the man tosses the mussel shells from the second batch out the train window as he eats them. The train has stopped on an overpass under which cars are travelling along the shore road. The young peddler leans from the window and sees that his shells are falling onto the road below. The *simit* seller exchanges meaningful looks with his brother and then turns to the customer.

"Sir, please, don't throw the shells out the window! Look, they're dropping on the cars."

A few voices in the car rise in support of the mussel seller and an elderly woman turns angrily towards the customer. "Aren't you ashamed of yourself?" she says. "You're polluting the environment. Look, the mussel seller has hung a bag on his stand. Throw them in there!"

"You're right, Teyze, but they take those empty shells home and restuff them again to sell the next day. Don't you have any idea of what's going on in this world?"

The mussel seller and his brother again exchange looks. He is preparing a defense in his head.

"Who says? Don't confuse me with those other types of mussel sellers!"

"Get off it! You're all alike anyway! Stuff "em and empty em and then crap on your customers!"

A voice issues from the back of the car, joining in on the argument. "Listen, *Abi*, if you're sure of all that, then why do you eat them?"

The customer turns in the direction of the voice and retorts, "Do I need your permission?" His anger is contagious and soon spreads through the car.

"Then don't throw those shells out the window!"

The train is now pulling into the Kumkapı Station and the two peddler brothers exchange eye signals to get off the train. Suddenly the customer hits the mussel peddler with a strong blow to his back, drawing loud protests throughout the car. The mussel seller has just pushed his way through the crowd to the open door when the customer also tries to give his mussel tray a swift kick. Although the man's kick misses its target, the peddler loses at least seven or eight stuffed mussels in his state of panic. The fallen mussels tumble onto the tracks. Before the train comes to a complete stop, the mussel seller jumps expertly to the ground and calls to his brother who is standing in front of the other train door, "Musto, get out of here! The inspector's coming!"

In a flash the inspector has Musto by the collar and off the train and then pulls him by his arm to a corner, delivering two swift blows at the same time. The train has now come to a complete stop and crowds of passengers are pushing on and off the train. The mussel customer stands in front of the door, happily watching Musto getting beaten. Musto, though, manages to free himself from the inspector's grasp and takes off running in the direction of the departing train, shouting loudly at the mussel eater, "Son of a whore, *kibrağı*! Son of a whore, *kibrağı*!"

RAT TRAP

Çınarlı Street echoed with the sounds of feet moving quickly along the pavement, sounds that would be drowned out completely, erased in the color of the night mixed with the rain, swallowed up by the sounds of conversation. The rain fell like nails and then merged with the silvery pools of running water as they met the hard asphalt. The windows in the houses clouded over and with the shadows they projected onto curtains, the weak light of lamps reflected fantastic images onto the street.

The owner of the grocery store, the Mercan Market, which stood directly opposite the centuries old plane tree that gave the street its name, was Boğos *Efendi*, a man widely known for his stinginess. After lowering the shop's security shutter, the grocer carefully clasped shut its padlocks. It had been at least three years since he had oiled the shutter and its strident screech as he pulled it down into place both interrupted the sound of the rain and caused those living nearby to invoke curses on the miserly grocer. He kicked the cigarette butts and candy wrappers in front of his door into the gutter and watched as the rain carried them down the street. Like always, as he had done for the past twenty-two years, he turned to look carefully at his shop before he set off into the night.

His spindly form was washed by the pale streetlight together with the rain beating down upon him, but his face lost none of its hard expression of greed. Beneath the warm streaks of the light boring through the darkness, he finally realized it was raining once the water began to drip down his head and onto his face. It was ten thirty as he set off with quick steps for his home.

It was only a short time later he reappeared beneath the same street lamp. The grocer was sopping wet now as he stuck the key back into the lock and pulled up the shop shutter. He swiftly stepped inside, turned on the lights, and proceeded to remove a large box of cookies from an upper shelf. Just then, a huge rat shot out from among the items on the shelf.

"God damn you! Tonight is going to be the end of you! Just who do you think you're playing with?"

From under the box he removed a money-filled packet wrapped up in newspaper. The packet looked the same as he had left it.

"Thank God nothing has happened to the money."

He relaxed a bit now.

He pulled the large sacks of bulgur and rice away from the wall and then lay down alongside his display refrigerator, sticking his arm under it as far as he could reach. His fingers found what they were looking for, but he had a hard time getting a grip on the item. By the time he was finally able to grasp the half-meter long iron rod, his face had become deeply flushed. An avaricious smile appeared on his face.

From the refrigerator he removed a block of feta cheese from the brine, letting its water drip sloppily onto the floor. He then neatly cut the cheese into two equal portions. Surprisingly, the stingy man was willing to forego this chunk of cheese, which he every day weighed precisely to the gram for his customers, to hunt down a rat.

The neighborhood knew about the rat. Housewives who had found rat droppings among their groceries had started to shop elsewhere. Even worse, a few times each and every day the neighborhood children would line up in front of his shop and shout in one voice, "Rat Grocery! Rat Grocery," just to anger the stingy grocer. Although he could turn a deaf ear to the complaints of the housewives, the children's shouting was driving him absolutely mad. Of the children, the one with the shrillest voice was Hüseyin's son, Ömer. Ten years earlier he and Hüseyin had formed a partnership to convert the grocery store into a market, but then the grocer had managed to squeeze Hüseyin out of the deal. Ömer's was the dominant voice. Or so it seemed to him...

Outside, lightening bolts were flashing across the sky. Boğos *Efendi* kept reassuring himself that tonight was the night to finish off the rat. From his pocket he removed an electric cable, then used the knife, now smeared in cheese, to scrape off some of the plastic covering it. Next he wrapped the exposed wires around one end of the iron pipe and bent its tip to secure it. He placed two layers of plastic sheeting under the pipe, insulating the pipe from the wooden floor. He put the block of cheese between the plastic and the pipe. Just as he was screwing up every gram of courage in his body to push the two exposed wires at the other end of the cable into the wall plug, the rustling sound coming from the sack of bulgur caused his rage at the rat to swell. A snapping noise or two came out of the cable as the wires made contact with the electricity. He used his circuit tester to check for electricity in the rod. Yes, everything was just as he wanted. The light of the circuit tester lit up, sparkling like a hero on his way to victory.

He looked around the shop one more time, picked up the package of money on the counter and carefully stuck it into his inside pocket. It was a little past midnight when he once again lowered the shop's shutter. The rain was beating down even harder now.

As he was standing in front of the door just getting ready to set off for home, he heard a woman's voice. The voice was coming from the third floor of the apartment building on the other side of the plane tree. When the woman saw Boğos Efendi, she stopped talking and called out to him.

"Good evening Boğos *Efendi*. What's up? You usually don't stay this late. Is anything wrong?"

Boğos *Efendi*'s reply was short and curt and implied that she was sticking her nose in his business, "There's nothing wrong! Good night!" he said as he turned on his heel.

The woman could not imagine any plausible reason why the grocer should be leaving at this hour. She followed him with her eyes until he turned the corner and passed from sight and then continued her conversation from where she had left off. As she talked, she continued to stuff a rag into the space around the window frame to mop up the rainwater that had seeped inside. The woman's name was Memnune, married these past thirty-nine years to alcoholic Hıdır, himself retired from his job on the Üsküdar-Eminönü ferry boat line.

When he was seventeen, Hıdır ran away from home and his rather well-to-do family, losing his inheritance in the process. He rode the rails on the back of trains until he was twenty-two and then, one year later, he ran off with Memnune. When faced with the need to earn a living, he managed to catch the Eminönü-Üsküdar ferryboat just in time for a ride that was to last a lifetime. He spent his youth and monthly salary on all of the fine points of alcohol, gambling, women, lies, and flat-out debauchery. In the process, he also managed to impregnate Memnune on four separate occasions. Now nearing the end of his life, he found himself alone with Memnune in a small house they had managed to come by, and with a pension of the sort about which everyone complains. The house was Memnune's inheritance from her father, while the pension was a symbol of the remains of opportunities Hıdır had missed.

His voice slurred with alcohol, Hıdır called out from an inner room.

"Shut that window. It's freezing in here. And hurry up, or I'll shut you up instead of the window."

Memnune had nothing to hide from the neighbors and so let their argument be heard by all through the open third floor window as she took out all of the rage she falt towards her husband on the window frame. How could the rainwater be at fault? If only her husband were a "thing" as clean as the water, that could be obliterated with the rag in her hand. And what was he good for now anyway? All those years... and for what? She turned to Hıdır.

"Just die right there where you're sitting, okay? Die so that I can be set free!"

To show that her words had absolutely no effect on him whatsoever, Hıdır rubbed his stomach in a calm and controlled manner.

"Don't get your hopes up. I have no intention of dying.

Now close that window!"

Memnune drifted off, watching the rain. But when a lightening bolt flashed, she felt suddenly afraid and wanted to run to Hıdır for comfort.

"To hope for help from a ship with only its mast left standing!"

"Stop muttering all that nonsense and get in here. And don't forget that this ship and its mast are still standing tall, afloat on the sea."

Memnune looked at the opposite corner and noticed that the next lightening bolt reflected against the light cast on the asphalt by the street light.

"If only that mast would be cast down so that I would be set free!"

She shut the window. They continued their conversation from inside.

The windows clouded over. She turned off the living room lights as the rain beaded down her windowsill.

The street was again left with only the rain for company. The only difference was that now a thin layer of smoke was seeping out from under Boğos *Efendi*'s shop shutter, meeting the rainwater coming in.

HAY ALLAH

She couldn't see the sea floor. "There'll be *lodos* today," she said in a quiet voice. It was so early in the morning that there was no one else about. She stuck her head out over the sea as far as she could but she was engulfed with a fear that a secret power would pull her into the water. She wondered what the depths of the sea would be like. There was so much filth floating on the top of the water that she thought maybe the floor of the sea would be nothing but a deep and muddy garbage pit that would swallow up every single cell of her body if she managed to venture down there. From her place on the shore, she suddenly dropped to her haunches and thought how helpless she was, and how inept.

She should go straight back. Maybe he wasn't dead after all....

No, she knew he was dead. She had touched his feet and had registered that they were cold, cold as ice, she thought. But what would she lose if she checked just one more time? Of course, if he hadn't been dead when she left him like that, he most certainly would be dead by now because at least eight hours had passed since she had last touched him. And how could it be her fault if he was dead? She had never thought that someone could be killed by being struck on the head by a flowerpot falling from a high place. And what's more, she never thought she could be involved in such a freak accident. She thought this kind of thing only happened in comic books. But that man had died after all! His dead body was lying just like that in the doorway to the backyard. Or maybe it wasn't really a dead body yet.

She remembered that she had left her key in the house.

"I can't get in the house!"

The whole affair had turned into a wave of events, a wave of events that had washed her up onto the shores of Kumkapı.

"*Hay Allah*, why in God's name did I ever make those stupid preserves?"

Everything that happened, yes everything, was the fault of that woman next door.

When she woke up that morning, she had felt a heavy weight pressing down on her. Children were again scurrying after each other on the street while the woman next door was shouting at them as loud as she could. The woman's screeching voice was driving her mad and so she went to the window to see what the fuss was all about.

"If only I hadn't looked out," she thought to herself.

The next-door neighbor was picking the figs that were ripening on the fig tree before the children could get to them. When the neighbor saw her looking from the window, she called for her to come down to get some of the figs. She did exactly what the neighbor suggested without raising any objections. She only managed to escape the children's pleading hands by promising that she would make them some fig preserves. Actually, she herself didn't like the taste of fig preserves. In one way she made the offer just to give the neighbor a needed lesson in generosity. Now there was no getting out of it. She had promised the children.

"If only I hadn't promised," she thought to herself.

She went back into her house and was actually happy that she had found a task that would keep her busy from morning to evening. By five in the afternoon, the preserves had cooked, so she took the pan off the fire and put it on the windowsill to cool.

"If only I hadn't put the pan out to cool," she thought to herself.

At around eight in the evening, she heard a noise and ran to the back of the house. She was very surprised to see that one of the brass pins holding the upper window sash in place had torn out and the other was hanging down, having allowed the upper window to lower. "Praise be to God," she said when she saw that her preserves hadn't fallen, but noticed that a plant that occupied the other end of the windowsill was no longer in its place.

"*Hay Allah*, and I just planted that geranium cutting!"

Anyway, the important thing was that nothing had happened to the preserves. She raised the window, holding it up with a stick. When she leaned out the window, she was shocked to see a man lying on the ground below the window. He was facedown and pieces of the broken flowerpot and clumps of soil were scattered on and around him.

"*Hay Allah*! Now look what's happened to me!"

She bit her tongue and had difficulty breathing. When she finally came to her senses, she understood that it was important that she not scream and so was happy she had bitten her tongue. It was now a quarter to nine as she moved haphazardly around the room, first in one direction and then another.

"*Hay Allah! Hay Allah!*" she repeated over and over again. All of a sudden she remembered her father.

"He's never this late," she thought to herself. "I wonder what's kept him. God forbid that something should happen to him."

She knew that she should go down and look at the man lying in the garden, but she was afraid of dead people. Now why did she think he was dead? She should go down right away because if he isn't dead then she should try to get him some help.

"But what if he is dead? I can't possibly ask any of the neighbors for help! The best thing is to wait for *Baba*."

It was ten by the time she decided to go down to the yard. At a quarter to eleven she was standing at the top of the stairs. Her body was stiff and it seemed that all of her bodily functions had stopped. She went down the stairs on the very tips of her toes. When she found herself standing in front of the garden door, she took a very deep and long breath. As she pushed the door open, the man's hand, which had been resting on the door, dropped to his leg. This caused her to scream. Then she grabbed the man and pulled him inside. The moment she had slammed the door shut, she realized that one of his shoes was still out in the yard.

"*Hay Allah!* It must have dropped off his foot when I pulled him inside."

She had to open the garden door a second time. By reaching out with her foot, she managed to drag the shoe inside the house. There were no tears in her eyes, yet her words came out as sobs as she muttered over and over again to herself. The man wasn't wearing any socks. She closed her eyes tight and forced herself to touch his foot.

"*Aman Allah*, his foot is icy cold. *Hay Allah*! He must be dead." She ground her teeth. "It can't be. No, no. He can't be dead! He can't! Don't be stupid! You're being stupid! Stupid! What's happening to me? His foot's cold. His foot's cold. His foot's cold."

She looked at her watch. It was eleven thirty. Suddenly she remembered her fig preserves on the windowsill. She ran upstairs and moved the preserves from the window to the very center of the table in the living room. The windowsill was sticky to the touch when she picked up the preserves. She ran up the stairs two and three steps at a time to get a rag from the kitchen in the middle floor and then ran down again. She was out of breath.

"What's kept him? He's never late. He always lets me know if he's going to go out drinking. *Hay Allah*! Should I tell the neighbors? What should I do?"

As she began to wipe the windowsill with the wet rag, she found herself stopping cold.

"*Hay Allah*," she said, "What about the man downstairs? No, he must still be there."

She went back downstairs. He was still there. As she was wondering what she should, the idea of taking the man back out to the garden and dragging him to the woodshed suddenly popped into her head.

But what about the neighbors?

"This is the rear end of the house and at this hour all of the neighbors have either gone to bed or are getting ready to," she thought.

"Why in earth's name did that woman give me the figs? And why in heaven's name did I have to please the children by promising them preserves? To teach the woman a lesson! *Hay Allah! Hay Allah!* Do you see now what you've done to yourself?"

As she smoothed her skirt into place, she realized that it was sticky with some of the preserves' syrup. She ran back upstairs, got a clean rag from the kitchen, wet it, and wiped furiously at her skirt. Some of the syrup was on her finger and when she licked it off she thought that it tasted very good. She got a small bowl and a fork and took them downstairs. She chose the plumpest of the figs from the pan of preserves sitting in the middle of the table in the living room. Then she pulled out a chair, sat down, and ate her full of the preserves. The figs were a kind of secret potion, sending an order to her brain to relax her body. And then the potion lost its power.

"*Hay Allah.* The man is downstairs."

She went back downstairs but could not draw up the courage to touch him. She knew, though, that she should pull him through the garden and lock him into the woodshed.

It was one in the morning when she locked the garden door from inside.

"*Hay Allah!* What if he's not dead and he dies after I stuff him into the woodshed? Won't I bear a burden of guilt all of my life?" she asked herself. "No, no, I should take him to a doctor. Or would it be better if I called a doctor to come here?"

She took the man back out of the woodshed, back into the house, and into the hall inside the garden door.

"What did I do? I don't even like fig preserves!"

It was five o'clock in the morning. Taking strength from the sun, the new day announced its coming by licking the sides of the buildings, which were softly red in the new light, starting from the bottom and slowly moving up. Some of the houses were already coming to life and a few laborers and clerks had already set out off for work. In other homes, the lights of those who were to leave a half an hour later were just coming on.

A deep feeling of weariness had invaded each of her bones. As she opened the drapes on the middle floor, she saw the son of the old lady across the street leave for his job as a garbage collector. She let the curtain quietly fall back into its place. When she went into the living room, a room facing the garden, she found herself preparing to take another fig from the pan on the table. "*Hay Allah!*" she said to herself. She went back upstairs to the kitchen and got a clean fork from the cutlery drawer. She used the clean fork to take another fig out of the pan and then started to eat the preserves with the fork she had used the night before. This was the sixteenth fig she had eaten.

"*Hay Allah*," she said. "What about the man downstairs? I need to get him out of the woodshed."

She took him out of the woodshed for the sixteenth time.

"If he hasn't died, I don't want to spend the rest of my life with a guilty conscience."

It was with labored steps that she climbed back up the stairs. She put on her raincoat and left the house.

"I didn't sleep a wink last night. Where could that man be? I'd better go to the police station and let them know he's missing. *Hay Allah*, now I think I've left my key in the house!"

Sure enough, when she put her hand into her pocket, she understood that she had indeed left the key at home. It was seven o'clock when she walked down to the shore.

The sun was shining now with all of its might. The waves

emphasized even more the paleness and weariness reflecting from her face. She watched the sea for a long time. Her stomach was burning unmercifully. She was thirsty and each wave hitting the shore deepened her thirst.

The sounds of feet woke her suddenly from the bed of stones on which she had fallen asleep.

"*Hay Allah*! What am I going to do now? Yes, yes, I need to go to the police station and turn myself in. I think I've killed someone. And, anyway, I can't commit suicide..."

For the first time she felt sure of herself. She immediately pulled herself together and set off for the police station.

At the station, she told the policeman on duty that she wanted to see the chief. When the policeman asked her what she wanted to see him about, she said that it was a matter about which she could talk to the chief only. The policeman, a man in his mid-thirties, was accustomed to these kinds of cases, but she didn't fit the pattern. Before him stood a woman neatly dressed in a raincoat, a woman with weary eyes and demeanor. He tried to imagine what could have happened to make this woman look like this, but the woman's constantly moving eyes and hands gave no clue. Her demeanor made even him curious. He showed her into the chief's office.

The chief offered the woman a seat. She was just about to sit down when she sprang to her feet.

"I've got to get home. I've left the preserves on the windowsill."

The chief asked her what preserves she was talking about.

"*Hay Allah*! I left the man in the woodshed."

"What man, Lady?"

The chief was beginning to get annoyed. He asked her what

she wanted and why she had come to the station. He then decided that she must be a little cracked in the head.

The woman began to speak in halting and short sentences.

"I made some preserves. I put the pan on the windowsill. The window fell. The flowerpot fell, too. A man was lying under the window, straight down. I went down. The man's feet were like ice. I put him in the woodshed. I didn't want him to die. Then I took him inside. Actually I don't like fig preserves. I just took one to check the taste. Honest to God, a person can't just eat something if he doesn't like it. I had a hard time eating that fig. You can't guess how my stomach is burning now. By the way, could I have a glass of water please? As you know, a sip of water will help somebody get something down if they don't liked what they've eaten."

She emptied the glass and continued to talk with her mouth full of water.

"I live with my father just two blocks away. My father is one of the famous fishermen around here."

The chief's face softened with recognition.

"You think I don't know him? Forget about eating enough fish to deplete the sea, we emptied many a wine barrel as well. And you're his daughter. How's he doing?"

The daughter paused for a moment.

"My father. He's just fine, this is the first time in all these years that he didn't come home. He didn't even send word that he wasn't coming! *Inşallah*, nothing bad has happened to him...."

Her face took on an expression of worry. She asked for another glass of water that she again drank in a single gulp. She took a deep breath and continued explaining.

"Actually, I think something bad has happened to me. God knows nothing like this has ever happened to me before. This is something that has never happened to anyone before, something unheard of. This is the first time in my life that I have ever left home without my keys. Even worse, I don't have any money on me to hire a locksmith because I forgot my wallet at home too!"

The chief of police turned and faced the woman with an expression that was at once sad and surprised, but comforting as well.

"*Hay Allah*! *Hay Allah*! All these problems! Well, you don't worry your sweet head about it. We'll sort this out for you right away."

THE NEW BRIDE

Softly licking against the drapes, the hot wind blew into the room. The August sun, sifting through water-saturated clouds, became a ball of fire that beat down on the wooden houses, on the jumbas, and onto the cobbled pavements along Cilavcı Street in Kumkapı.

An elderly man sat on a divan in front of an open window, slowly spinning the cigarette he held between the fingers of his left hand. He hated the hot wind but he didn't want to close the window.

"For days now it just can't make up its mind whether to rain or not; if only it would rain and we could be saved from this heat," he murmured with displeasure.

He became even more irritated by the squeaking noise of the wheels of the watermelon truck as it drew near his house. Now parked under his window, its squeaking had mercifully stopped but now the peddler began to call out from his loudspeaker. The old man angrily slammed his window shut. The ashes from his cigarette dropped onto the living room rug but he put out the embers with one of his leather-soled slippers. The room soon filled with the odor of onions being fried for the evening meal. Watermelon noise outside and onion smell inside — he was ready to explode.

The voice calling out from the kitchen diminished some of his anger.

"*Baba*, if you're hungry, the food will be ready in just a half an hour."

Rather than answering in a normal tone, he had an urge to shout out the fact that he was indeed hungry. He had become a spoiled child who complained above everything.

He met his urge with one simple loud "Noooo!"

This response drew Vartanuş into the room.

"What's wrong *Baba*? You've been sitting here upset for several days now. Aren't you going to tell us what's bothering you? You're making us upset, too. If you can't talk to me, then at least talk to Artin."

Actually, for some time now he had been thinking about talking to his son, but he just couldn't bring himself to do so. Of course he would explain the matter first to Vartanuş, but the matter would only be solved after she relayed it on to Artin. It was now high time, and time was even ticking by. He rubbed his fingers against the worn cloth of his jacket. Since his daughter-in-law couldn't see the thinness of the fabric from where she stood, he decided not to use it as a source of complaint, but then his eyes lit upon a stain on his trousers.

"I'm a mess. I haven't even got a clean pair of pants. The clothes I wear are no better than burlap bags! And with all the wealth here...."

Vartanuş couldn't imagine the direction her father-in-law was trying to take the conversation.

"That's right, Baba, but whenever we try to get you to buy new clothes, you're the one who refuses to do so! Why are you bringing this up now?"

He paused.

"If this is what's worrying you, we can go out tomorrow and buy you new clothes," Vartanuş continued.

The old man turned his face towards the window and began to mutter to himself.

"Oh ho! If only my problems could be solved with a new jacket and trousers! For God's sake, what person can be made happy with a bolt of cloth?"

The matter was on the very tip of his tongue and he felt like he would explode with its weight. Just as he was going to get it out, Vartanuş turned on her heel and ran back to the kitchen. When she got back, joy radiated from her face at having saved the meal. She walked towards the window.

"Do you want me to open the window? Let's let some fresh air into the room!"

She got no response. The watermelon truck was gone now, so, before his daughter-in-law could do so, he jumped up to open the window himself. He first bent over to straighten his slipper. In a display of respect, Vartanuş also moved to straighten his slipper and noticed ashes sticking to its bottom. It was the sight of the new burn spot on the rug, though, that brought a frown to her face. She turned on her heel and went back into the kitchen without saying a word. She was determined now to put off asking her father-in-law about what it was that was bothering him. The old man opened the window and sat back down on the divan.

His eyes fell on the burn spot. He felt pleased having gotten his revenge for not being able to talk about his problems with his daughter-in-law by damaging the rug.

"Oh, that was a good one!"

He grabbed his jacket and went outside, but then stopped abruptly after taking only three or four steps.

"Am I getting rusty, or what? Sitting at home all the time is making me go soft. This isn't the way at all. Everybody else is out having a good time, while I - a man after all- don't even let myself go to the coffeehouse."

At the end of the street he turned down Balipaşa Hill. It wouldn't be long before the sun set. He could make out the waves on the sea from the very top of the hill. The little waves rose to fly and then beat their wings at each other in play among the white froth of the sea, tumbling with joy to the shore.

"The sea has gone rabid," he said to himself.

The tailor Ohannes was just coming out of his shop to retrieve the coal-heated iron he had left outside to cool. The last rays of the sun were struggling to keep their power as they pierced the shop window after bouncing off Kirkor's eyeglasses. "Kirkor, come on in and drink a glass of tea," called Ohannes.

He went into the shop and the two men chatted about ordinary events as they sipped their teas. Kirkor pulled back out of view when he caught sight of Vartanuş's brother Dikran walking down the hill. But he was too late; Dikran had already seen him, nodded a hello, and was about to turn the knob to enter the shop.

"Selamünaleykümüne Kirkor Dayday.

Kirkor did not bother to respond to the Arabic greeting but remained seated and silent. He tried to look like he was working by picking up one of Ohannes' half-finished jackets and starting to play around with the basting along the collar edge. Looking over the rims of his glasses, he uttered a Turkish greeting, "*Hoş geldin.*" He didn't like Dikran. As far as he was concerned, Dikran had every single negative quality that a person could possibly have.

"What kind of a greeting is that? What do you mean by, 'Selamünaleykümüne Kirkor Dayday'?"

"Is it a crime for me to greet you with a '*selam*' Kirkor Dayday?" was Dikran's irritated rebuff.

"Your excuse is even worse than your crime. If you're going to talk like that, you might as well add a *Hacı* after my name instead of calling me uncle. Is that any kind of talk for an Armenian?"

"Don't get mad, *Dayday*. I was only trying to kid you a little because I know you don't like it."

"Well, listen, blabbermouth, I don't like you talking to me in that messed up Kumkapı slang."

"If I have made a mistake in your eyes, *Dayday*, then please forgive me. So, I'm sorry. Anyway, let's drop it. What do you say that some evening me and Verjin and the kids come over to your place? We'll bring a couple fish from the shore and set up a *çilingir* table and we can eat *meze*.

Kirkor now knew why the slacker Dikran was trying so hard to be friendly. The bum was such a freeloader that he had no shame whatsoever. He could pretend to be friendly just to get something for free, especially from Kirkor who was in no mood at the moment to say no to anything; he'd even take the old man's underpants if he could. So long as he could remember, Kirkor had been able to hold his own, but now Dikran was holding a trump card. For eight months now he had been playing with the old man, the same way a cat plays with a mouse. Their seeming friendliness had sparked everyone's curiosity, but no one had asked Kirkor or Dikran the reason behind it. On several occasions his wife had been on the verge of asking, but Dikran had always managed to change the subject before she had the chance. For years they had studiously ignored each other, but for the past eight months now they acted like the very best of friends. It was obvious that Kirkor had tired of the game.

"I don't know anything about that. You'd better tell Artin and Vartanuş what you want. It's not anything to worry me about," he told the thick-skinned Dikran.

Kirkor rose to his feet and said to Ohannes, "It would take at least forty witnesses to prove that this Dikran is Vartanuş' brother." He then walked out of the shop and continued on his way down the hill.

The last rays of the sun were getting ready to desert Balipaşa Hill for the night. The wings of the waves playing in the froth seemed to have grown tired. The sea had put on its dark evening clothes and seemed to be telling the waves, "Okay kids, that's enough for today, now it's my turn to play," as it got ready for its own wild performance.

Kirkor stopped in his tracks. He sensed Dikran walking behind him. When he turned around he saw that he had not been mistaken.

"Listen to me, Dikran, you're beginning to be too much! Is it a crime for someone to want to get married? Go and tell whoever it is you want to tell. Don't forget that it is not immoral to get married. What you're doing is immoral. You're blackmailing me and you better be careful that I don't catch you up to something!"

He spat out the words in rapid order and with decisiveness.

His body was stiff with emotion and as the words shot out of his mouth, he felt that his very marrow had been drained. It had been a very long time since he had been so angry.

Whistling now, Dikran passed by Kirkor with impudence.

"Why this nasty mood, Old Man, just for a few measly bucks. You know there wouldn't be any problem if you'd just let me get a little whiff of that fortune you're sitting on." Having said this, Dikran turned into Şükrü's coffeehouse when he got to the corner.

Kirkor was wet through and through with perspiration. He went back home.

Vartanuş was sitting at the table snapping a bowl of beans. She raised her eyes when she saw her father-in-law enter but her hands continued with their task.

"What's happened, *Baba*? Did you walk a long way? You seem tired."

"What do you mean, 'tired?' I'm not tired; it's just that I ran into that blabbermouth brother of yours. If it weren't for you, I know what I'd show him, but then you'd be in the middle."

He stood up so as not to have to look at the frown clouding Vartanuş' face. "I'am going to taking a nap," he said as he walked toward his room.

Artin was home and the evening meal was ready to be eaten. He had already heard about the day's events. After dinner he turned to his father.

"Baba, let's go for a little walk."

Kirkor suggested they go to a *meyhane*.

"What's up Baba? You want to drink?"

"Let's drink together."

They went out. It was raining hard outside.

"Hay, for the life of your father!" the old man thought to himself. "I wouldn't care a bit if a flood carried everything away." Then remembering his son walking next to him, he turned to look at him and say,

"Don't look at me like that. Just keep walking."

The rain had stopped by the time they got to the *meyhane*. The overriding heat of the day had given way to a sweet and calming coolness.

Kirkor took a sip of the icy cold *rakı*.

"Those were wonderful days."

"Which days, *Baba*?"

"The days when your mother would fix rakı meals. Do you remember? She used to make the most delicious meze."

"Of course I remember," replied Artin. An expression of longing passed over his face. It must have been longing for his mother that had inspired tonight's drinking. He also took a drink of *rakı*, then downed the rest with a second gulp. His eyes misted over.

The old man turned to his son.

"You know your mother was very talented. And devoted. She dedicated her life to us, and to the house. If she were here today we wouldn't be in a place like this. We would be home drinking our *rakı* there. And I wouldn't have been a burden on you all this time. We would be living in our own house and you would be living in yours."

His face looked grieved.

Artin answered, "Don't talk like that, *Baba*. Is there anyone who's bothered by you?" The words had no sooner gotten out of his mouth than he noticed his father's expression change from a picture of sadness to that of a clever trap.

"No, no, why do you say that now son. Only today I acciden-tally burned the rug. Well, you know, these things happen and really she's an outsider...."

"*Baba*, you're not being fair."

"Ahhh, but anyway your mother died of grief over that sister of hers, that whore of a sister of hers."

"*Baba*, Mom fell down the stairs!"

Kirkor was becoming increasingly stubborn.

"Yeah, right, but I know that's what she was thinking about when she went down those stairs. If the one her sister ran away with had only been a real man. Okay, we accepted the fact that he was Moslem, but if he had been a doctor, an engineer, an architect, at least someone with a diploma... But no, he was a Moslem and the son of an imam - and a taxi driver to boot!"

Artin filled their glasses again. He looked at his father with pleading eyes that finally registered. Right, it was now the time to start talking about the real issue. Kirkor started out by talk-ing about inheritance.

"Listen, Artin. I don't know how much longer I am going to be on this earth. The two of you have set up your own lives and you're moving along. Ayy, the girls are growing up and they're going to study. You know that everything I have is going to them. And you know it's not that small a deal. The apartment in Cihangir, the house in Kumkapı, the apartment in Kurtuluş. It's all yours. In fact, as time goes on, you may even sell one of these and send the girls to get an education abroad."

Artin interrupted his father with a tired voice.

"*Baba*, the girls are studying very well right here as it is. And nobody has eyes on your property anyway. You just keep on living. Stay at the head of this family."

"Yeah I want to go on living and I want to stay at the head of this family, but I'm afraid that this loneliness is going to send me packing very soon."

Artin's expression was blank when he looked at his father's face.

"What are you trying to say?" he asked. He emptied his *rakı* glass for the second time.

The old man had his words out in a heartbeat. "I want to get married."

"What?? Married?? What??"

It seemed that the meyhane was closing in on Artin's head. He put his face close to his father's. The vein on his neck had popped out and his face was bright red.

"Listen to me. You're seventy-seven years old. Your skin is wrinkled like a prune's and your hair is white. You should be ashamed of yourself. Ashamed! I will never, ever accept such a thing! First of all, I will never accept a woman to succeed my mother. Second, I don't have the time, nor the money, to arrange for and pay for a funeral for some seventyyear-old bitch. And in memory of my mother! Don't say that you are even thinking about such a thing with even the very tips of your brain!"

Despite his son's heated reaction, the old man actually felt better. At least he had expressed his feelings. It was now his turn to reply.

"Who says I'm going to marry a seventy-year old"?

Artin's words shot out of his mouth like silver bullets, exploding throughout the *meyhane*.

"What?! Or have you got your eyes set on someone your daughter's age?"

The whole meyhane was looking at them now. Artin jumped to his feet.

"Yeah, marry a woman in her twenties and have a heart attack on your marriage bed! Let the whore who'd marry you eat up your inheritance!" he said, just before he marched out of the *meyhane*.

The men sitting in the meyhane begin to look at Kirkor with curious expressions. It was obvious that he couldn't sit there any longer. He paid the bill and set off for home. He talked to himself the whole way home.

"Look at that little bastard. Feed him, take care of him, raise him, and then see what happens... Anyway, what can I say? It's fate. Fate. My wife dies and then I'm left alone with all my money. That donkey, son-of-a-donkey! Is that what my fate has to be? Makes me look like a fool and then he gets up and leaves me there. At least that's what everybody in the *meyhane* thought. Look what that donkey, son-of-a-donkey did! I don't know who that devil takes after! Look what I'm wondering about! Wondering when I already know the answer. Who else could he take after? Of course he took after that no-good brother of mine, after Suren. See, see here Suren what you've done? From this day on I will never do another *hokehankist* or give money to the poor and needy in your name. Anyway, I never wanted to do so in the first place. There, you know it now. You left your money to your nephew and see what you did! Look what that bastard has done! That son of a bitch! Look what he's done."

Kirkor got home to find that the house had settled into a deep silence, a silence that was to last a long time. But there was no turning back now. The beans had been spilled. The old peace and contentment of the house was gone. It was obvious that he should move out and it wouldn't be a bad idea to have a smartly dressed woman hanging onto his arm as he did so. He knew, though, that the longer he put off acting, the more difficult it was going to be.

Autumn and winter came and went. Spring was upon them. It was the kind of spring day that the new season tries to hold tightly to, a day with a sweet coolness to the air. Everyone found themselves out of doors with people touching shoulder to shoulder as they passed in the narrow streets squeezed between their wooden houses. Windows were flung open and curtains, inebriated with the nectars of the season, danced in the breezes.

From where he sat, the old man muttered to himself, "Yes, spring, it will be this spring."

He summoned his daughter-in-law Vartanuş to his side and after taking a deep breath got up the courage to say,

"You know that I have decided to get married."

"Yes I know, Baba," she replied. She thought to herself that her father-in-law was becoming more and more pigheaded.

"We thought, though, that you had given up on the idea. So I guess that means that you haven't," she said with a strange smile.

"That son-of-a-bitch husband of yours hasn't even said a decent word to me for the past three months. That shameless bastard! And am I supposed to act like a father to him? I don't have to ask him for permission to get married! I only talked to him about it out of a sense of decency. We're a family and I didn't want us harboring secrets. As if I had to ask his permission before I married his mother!"

The old man continued with pleading eyes.

"Look, Vartanuş, whatever happens, you'll always be like a daughter to me. I want you to know how much you mean..."

Vartanuş injected, "Thanks, *Baba*, but you don't have to say anything."

"You're the only person who understands me. You know what they say: 'Let the male nation dry up!' So, there it is. Whatever is good in this world, it's because of women. You're the only person in this world who will help me."

So saying, he left Vartanuş with no escape.

"All right. I'll talk to Artin."

Now the old man was suddenly frightened.

"Oh no, for the love of God, don't do that! I know that devil! He's stubborn. But as he is my son so am I his father. I'll be even more stubborn. Yeah, but I know where he got it; he got his stubborn streak from Suren."

This caused Vartanuş to get angry.

"Stop it *Baba*. Uncle Suren's dead and gone; let him at least rest in peace.

Kirkor raised one eyebrow and looked quizzically at Vartanuş.

"Have you forgotten so fast what he did to your mother?"

"Lord, this man is strange," thought Vartanuş. He kept opening old journals that should have been left closed years ago. And now he was trying to bargain with her in a very odd fashion.

"Leave off it, *Baba*. What's happened has happened. It's all water under the bridge now. So just tell me what it is you want."

The old man settled back into his armchair.

"What I want is for you to listen to me now. You know that Razmik, the one that lives near the train station on the same side of the street as the cream man Moris? You know, the daughter-in-law of the pickle maker? Her sister Mari looks like she's got a straight head."

Vartanuş' eyes opened wide like fortune-telling stones.

"What are you saying, Baba? That Mari is only thirty-five at the most! That's unthinkable!"

"No, no, it's not unthinkable... don't jump to conclusions right away."

He was holding a very strong trump card.

"Her husband died in a traffic accident, didn't he?"

"Yes, that's right."

"And as far as I've heard, she was left with three kids. She's a woman with principles. Good for her. She goes out and cleans other people's houses and she's doing her best to get her children educated."

Vartanuş shook her head with disbelief. She was trying to figure out what direction this talk was going to take him.

"So, I'll make her a queen in my house. I'll make her the crown on my head and I'll make her children the precious stones to wear in that crown."

Vartanuş was shocked.

"That's all well and good, *Baba*, but I can't go to their door with a proposal like that. I'll be humiliated. If you want her so bad, you can go and ask, but I won't do it!"

She shook her head from side to side. She was entirely taken aback by her father-in-law's insistent pleas for a woman and she could not help but feel disgusted by him. She was sorry she ever gotten into this conversation with him, but now there was no turning back. Even if she refused to help her father-in-law, she still had to talk him out of wanting to marry Razmik's sister. "God forbid that Mari should ever hear of this for she would be devastated," she thought to herself as she also envisioned the humiliation her own family would feel.

"Why don't you forget about Mari, *Baba*? I'll tell you what, just for you, just to make you happy, I'll talk to Razmik about Hiripsime, the widow of the pickle-maker. You know, her husband died two years ago."

"Mari needs a husband, a husband with money," was Kirkor's only reply.

This means he was intent on starting a serious bargaining process with his daughter-in-law. It also meant that he had his heart and mind set on Mari.

"It's up to you, Baba! But I'll take no part in this."

"You just don't say anything to Artin about this, that's all I want from you" Kirkor replied

"Fine *Baba*. You know Artin has a fit when he hears the least little thing about this topic anyway!"

There was no way out for Vartanuş. Kirkor had backed her securely into a corner. She took a deep breath as she replied,

"God give me patience! Anyway, let me see what I can do."

Two weeks later the old man was sitting in his usual spot in front of the open window. As he watched the people going by, now and then exchanging pleasantries with those he knew, he also spun his favorite fantasy in his mind. He was happy. His grandchildren were playing inside and he was pleased to get news from old friends. How bright everything looked! How full of hope for the future! He didn't stop to ask the source of his happiness, but only whispered, over and over again, "How sweet. How sweet."

It was just at this point that he spotted Artin turning the corner into their street. The sweetness turned to a bitter taste in his mouth. He had the uneasy feeling that his son could read his thoughts as he quickly tried to erase the fantasy that had been giving him so much pleasure. After all, the dreamer and the spy both knew one another intimately. He was overcome with guilt at these thoughts of his - thoughts he could hardly admit even to himself that he was having - each time "the spy" caught him at it. Just like now...

Artin was carrying a briefcase in one hand and a bag of groceries in the other as he walked up to the open window. He studied the old man before speaking and saw the change in his father's demeanor. It was in vain that the old man tried to act as if nothing had happened

"I see you are in your place at the window, *Müsü* Kirkor," Artin called out.

The older didn't bother to answer. The bubble of the dream had burst and Kirkor was again an old man living with his son. "Who am I to dream of getting married?" he murmured under his breath.

He didn't believe this statement himself, but just the saying of it evoked a certain sadness. At least he had succeeded in affecting Artin.

By the time Artin came into the house the old man had closed the window and retired to his room.

Artin reopened the window and sat in his father's place. He thought about how much he loved this street. He had been born here and grew up here. His eyes turned to the Gedikpaşa Hill that stretched down from his street. The street had borne witness to all of the happenings of the neighborhood. It had dropped a tear for each change of cobblestones. He looked at the house on the other side of the street and remembered Bercuhi. How he had loved her! She and her father lived on the top floor of that house. Every neighborhood has one beauty and she was this neighborhood's beauty! He let his eyes slide to the corner. This is where Bercuhi's father had his fruit and vegetable stand. They used to call Bercuhi the "peddler's daughter." *Müsü* Hamparsun didn't even wink an eye the day he sent his daughter as a bride to America, and from that day on Artin had hated the peddler. He never again spoke a word of greeting to the man nor did he even buy a single green bean from his stand. But hey, Bercuhi was happy enough to go to America. After all, it was America! Even Artin had exaggerated ideas about America. And even though he loved Bercuhi so much, he understood why she chose to go. He thought that having the chance to go to America was like winning the lottery and Bercuhi just happened to hold the winning ticket. His Uncle Suren was instrumental in helping him get over this idea. He did it with two fast slaps on his face.

"You idiot! And you call yourself a man? Why have you fallen under this 'American spell'? So much under the spell that you let that beautiful thing get away! Okay, so the girl is stupid. That's another matter. But what's wrong with you? Everybody always thinks that these places they haven't seen are somehow better than what's before them! Who's to blame her? You would have done the same thing if you had the chance. Who's been able to keep their ass tied down that I should expect you to? Get over here in front of me! Now!"

Artin was afraid of his uncle's eyes, sparking out flames. Artin was like a street cat hiding in a corner, afraid to come out. After licking his wounds for a few days, Artin thought that his Uncle Suren was probably right.

"Who's been able to keep his ass tied down that..."

He paused and let his eyes go back to the corner where the Bercuhi's father sold his vegetables.

"Nothing stays the same. Especially people. Our asses can't stay in one place but sooner or later the black earth finds us, wherever we are, and swallows us up. If only the peddler hadn't died, and if only his corner weren't empty..."

After Bercuhi left for the States, her father didn't live long. He immigrated, too - to the other world. Five years later, the new residents of their old apartment, Azniv Hanım and her family, immigrated to France, leaving only their daughter Vartanuş behind and that only because she had married Artin. The mother begged her daughter and son-in-law to come with them. Vartanuş and her father-in-law were willing to make the move but both Suren and Artin were set against it. Artin never forgot the telephone conversation that took place between his uncle and his mother-in-law. On her end of the call Azniv *Hanım* was blaming Suren. Though Uncle Suren first tried to keep a pleasant tone to his voice, it wasn't long before his words became fiery points that drove hot spears into Azniv's soul. That was the last conversation that was ever to take place between the two before they each departed this world, Azniv *Hanım* in France and Uncle Suren in Turkey.

"Listen to me, you can go and live among those strangers, but you have no right to force others to do the same! You just stay put and just maybe one day you'll learn enough French to even count yourself as one of them! And even if you don't, then maybe when you die you can at least go to a Frenchman's heaven!"

Azniv's angry reply at the other end of the receiver was so loud that it echoed throughout the room. She was especially mad at Suren for having the nerve to talk about death, and her death at that.

"You die! Why should I?"

"Yes, I will die! I'm not afraid of death... Death should be afraid of me! After all, I'm going to lie in my own country. The meadows of Muş will extend beyond my feet. There'll be a mulberry tree at my head and when the wind blows the birds that come for the leaves will greet me. Listen to me Azniv Hanım, if you had stayed here you'd be fit to lie in the ground of Balıklı Cemetery, but no, the dirt of France suits you better!"

After slamming down the phone, he turned and looked into Vartanuş' weeping eyes. He was immediately sorry for his strong language and apologized profusely to his nephew's wife. He added quietly that he had only spoken for himself and that everyone·else was free to go to France if they so desired.

Artin loved his Uncle Suren. Throughout his life, Artin measured all of his actions against his uncle's and, when faced with any hard decision, would ask himself what his uncle would have done in this kind of situation.

Everyone knew how much Uncle Suren loved Daron, the city called Muş by the Turks. He had been born there but was so young when he left that he had no recollection of it whatsoever. His family had moved to Istanbul when he was still in swaddling clothes. Still, he always said that a secret power drew him to Muş. Artin was very curious about this secret power that he only solved years later when he himself had become an adult. Everyone, he understood, feels a longing for the land of his birth. This longing becomes greater upon separation from the land. The longing only intensifies and never weakens. The longing that Uncle Suren had for the lands of Muş grew stronger and stronger through the years. His heart beat for Muş. And as the years passed, the longing for Muş was transformed into an overwhelming love. Whenever he got that faraway look in his eyes, Artin knew what his uncle was dreaming of. His eyes would become misty and his lips would tighten into an expression of grief. His face became a map of Muş and he would dip in and out of the map. Whenever he snapped back out of his fantasy he would murmur the poem recited so often by his own father, Keğam:

"Who comes after the young hero?

Let whoever comes, come, Keğam, my man!

To the meadows of Muş! The beautiful meadows of Muş!

Go and ask my brother. Is there grief and longing there?

They ask the place where the fire drops from my eyes,

That fire drops on the meadows of Muş.

Go and turn the road around. The fire is a river now.

Ask it, ask it if it knows the man, the man Keğam.

The fire drops from my eyes but doesn't know the place.

I know but I do not tell.

The river swells and carries me, deep under the tree.

Jesus knows and so does Mary,

I worm among the tree roots and flow out, out into the meadows of Muş."

His uncle recited this poem so often that Artin had memorized it. He always told Artin, "This is the only inheritance I leave you." And now he lay in the Balıklı cemetery.

Artin's face reflected sorrow as he thought of his uncle lying in Istanbul.

"At least he's not in some cemetery in a foreign land," he thought. "If only I had inherited just a little bit of his spunk, then I could have turned down this dirty wish of my father's. The devil tells me just to go ahead and let him get married. You just can't make a person like this stay true to his memories! Gone! Gone away! My mother is gone and all memories of her are gone! Let him get married then."

That night he told his father what he had decided. He said it without looking at his father's face and he said it as if the words held no meaning whatsoever.

As soon as Dikran heard the news, he was back at the door of the house, out of breath and breathing hard. He didn't wait for the old man to welcome him into the house but pushed through the door with excitement. His eyes were shining.

"Listen, old man, if anyone can do something, it's me. I found a girl for you."

The old man stood up straighter. At first he thought that Dikran was teasing him, but then he saw that the younger man was very serious.

"The girl's from Samandağ in Hatay. She's twenty-eight. And she's right good looking, too!"

The old man's eyes took on a gleam.

"Is she divorced? Or a widow?"

"No, listen now Old Man: She's a virgin! A virgin!" His words took on the tone and the melody of a peddler's prattle. "We're going to go to Samandağ and get her with a real celebration."

Kirkor's heart started beating fast.

"You want money? Money, right? You don't even breathe for free!"

"Don't talk to me of money. This is my gift to you. So what do you say?"

"Let's do it. Let's do it now!"

Two weeks later Kirkor, Vartanuş, Dikran and his wife, Verjin, all went to Hatay together. They did as the old man bid and put on a very ostentatious wedding, bringing the new bride back to Istanbul with them. Both of her arms were covered with gold bracelets. She was a walking jewelry shop, not to mention those jewels she had packed into her hope chest.

They moved into the Kurtuluş apartment. The old man was very happy. Artin, though, had completely broken off relations with his father. It nauseated him just to drive through the neighborhood in which his father now lived, let alone take his name into his mouth.

A few months later the old man walked into the old neighborhood with a hero's stride. Color had returned to his cheeks. His clothes were clean and his shoes highly polished. He looked much younger. He turned a deaf ear to the whispers of his former neighbors as he strode into his son's apartment building.

His relationship with Vartanuş had remained the same as always. Since he married he had gotten much closer to her brother Dikran and sometimes Vartanuş even visited them in Kurtuluş, without of course informing her husband. This time Kirkor had something important to discuss with his daughter-in-law, so he came to her house rather than waiting for her to visit his. He sat in his regular place and only began to speak when his daughter-in-law had brought him his tiny cup of Turkish coffee.

"Daughter," he said, "I am very happy with my life and, in a sense, I owe this all to you. I am so lucky that God sent a person like you and your brother to me, people who have drunk of unsullied mother's milk."

Vartanuş cut him off with a modest, "You don't have to say such things, *Baba*." She knew there was something he was hiding under his tongue.

Kirkor didn't wait long to get it out.

"I've got very good news. Ankine's pregnant."

The words were hardly out when Vartanuş let out a little scream.

"What??!! Now you've gone too far, *Baba*. At this age.... God forbid that Artin should hear of this. Whatever you do, do, but don't rob this house of its peace!"

Kirkor didn't wait to hear the rest of her response. He grabbed his hat, slammed the door, and marched out of the house without speaking.

It didn't take long for Artin to get wind of the matter. He set off at once for the house in Kurtuluş. A servant opened the door. The new couple was sitting on the balcony drinking tea. Artin pushed the servant aside and went out to the balcony. Seeing his son, the old man had to swallow the suddenly dry cookie in his throat. At first Artin said nothing but looked slowly at the old man and the young woman in her dressing gown and heavy gold jewelry.

"God, you must even sleep with your jewels!"

He felt like pushing her off the balcony but kept himself under control. He turned to his father, his eyes blazing.

"Are you planning on bringing me a brother to raise?"

He looked again at the young woman and then raised his finger and pointed it in his father's face.

"Listen, man, you'd better think twice. I am dead serious. Either I'll take my own life, or I won't care a bit about you as a father, and I'll kill someone else."

The strong words scared the old man who turned icy cold in his chair. His hands trembled as he spoke.

"Ankine's no longer pregnant. She miscarried last week."

His son was quick with his response.

115

"Let me just get the slightest whiff about anything to do with you and this nauseating wife of yours and I swear to you that I'll kill you both," he said before stomping out of the apartment.

The young woman was shocked.

After a long silence, the old man turned to Ankine.

"Sweetheart. Baby. My Little Bird... Look now what that bastard has done. He's crazy. He takes after that crazy uncle of his. I worked hard and made a fortune. I made money so that my family would be taken care of. Still, what was the good of it? And what did that bastard ever do? Left a poem as an inheritance! Tell that to anybody and they'd die laughing. And look what we've got today! One's in the grave and the other's gone raving mad. And he'll keep his promise, too! That devil!"

Ankine was confused as she tried to make sense of what her husband was saying. She turned to her husband.

"What are you trying to say?"

"I'm trying to say that I think we should find a doctor and abort that baby..."

The woman's eyes grew round and her face beet red as she pounded on the table.

"You better understand this right now. I don't care if the sky falls. I'm going to have this baby!"

The old man pleaded with his wife for days on end and with the help of a Trabzon-worked, braided gold bracelet finally managed to convince Ankine to abort the baby.

From that day on the pregnancies seemed to occur every few months or so and each time the old man managed to persuade his wife to trade the baby for a bauble or two. The visits from Ankine's relatives also became more frequent and they stayed for longer and longer periods of time. The husband and wife started to argue and the old man lost his contentment and peace. One day Ankine approached her husband in an innocent fashion. "I know you're tired of my family. I don't want their visits either. But what can I do? I feel so sorry for them. You know how difficult their lives are. I just don't have the conscience to throw them out. I was thinking that maybe we should get the renters out of the Cihangir flat and let them live there. Then when other relatives visit they can stay there and we can get the peace of our house back."

The old man breathed a deep sigh of relief and immediately accepted the idea. He wasn't quite sure how it happened, but the deed for the house shortly passed into his wife's name as well.

The young woman started traveling back and forth between their house and the Cihangir apartment and sometimes she spent days, and then weeks at time staying with her relatives. Old Kirkor was once again home alone.

"I just can't take this life," he thought. "When she comes back, I'm going to sit down and have a very serious discussion with her. She'd better understand that I am no husband to be left alone!"

Another week went by but his wife still didn't appear. Kirkor decided to take matters into his own hands and go and bring his wife home. Anyway, the situation couldn't be any worse than it was now.

When he got to the flat he rang the bell.

He was gathering all his courage together and framing his words when the door was opened.

The door was opened by someone he had never seen before. Boiling water seemed to suddenly pour over his head. He didn't even have the opportunity to ask who it was when the man himself supplied the answer. He said they were the new owners of the flat, that they had bought it two months ago and moved in ten days earlier.

The new owner turned to the old man.

"Do you know Dikran Bey? I bought it from him. It was his wife's house. They decided to move to France. We got it pretty cheap, that's for sure."

"Great God in heaven," murmured the old man as he sank slowly to the pavement.

GUIDE TO PRONUNCIATION

For proper names and some other words in this book, original Turkish spelling has been used. The following is a short guide to pronouncing these words.

Vowels in Turkish are pronounced as in French or German:
a - as in father
e - as in met
i - as in big
o - between the o in role or the au in author
u - as in rule

In addition, there are three other vowels that do not occur in English:

ı - undotted i, pronounced as the vowel sound in the second syllables of words such as herbal or function
ö - as in German
ü - as in German

Consonants are pronounced as in English, except for the following:

c - as j in jam, e.g. cami (mosque) = jahmy
ç - as ch in chat, e.g. çorba (soup) = chorba
g - as in get, never as in gem
ğ - is almost silent and tends to lengthen the preceding vowel
ş - as in sugar, e.g. çeşme (fountain) = cheshme

119

GLOSSARY

Abi: Short for ağabey (literally "older brother"), it is used as a polite form of expression for men in Turkish.

Abla: Literally, "older sister", but used as a polite form of expression for women in Turkish.

Allahumma enni auzubke mınal habsı vel habais: O God, protect me from Satan, the jinns, and all of their acts.

Aman Allah: Exclamation like "Oh God!"

Amca: Uncle.

Baba: Father.

Bacı: Term used when addressing a woman.

britlerine: Belt loops.

cirdon: Mouse (Kurdish).

çilingir: Literally "locksmith" but used as slang to identify a drinking table replete with food.

çük: Child's word for penis.

Daye: Mommy (Kurdish).

Dayday: Armenian variant of Turkish dayı (maternal uncle).

Dizgin Arat, ur es?: Miss Azat, where are you? (Armenian).

Efendi: Like "sir," but used with the first name.

gor: Diyarbakır slang. Actually Persian for "grave."

Hacı: Islamic term of respect added after the name of the person who has made the sacred pilgrimmage to Mecca.

Hanım: Term used together with the first name to formally address a woman.

Hay: Armenian (Armenian).

GLOSSARY

hay Allah: Exclamation like "Oh God!"

he, hee: Slang for yes (Kurdish).

Hisus Kristosus: Jesus Christ.

hokehankist: Prayer ceremony for the dead.

Hos em Kayane, yegur!: Here I am, come here! (Armenian).

Hoşgeldin: Words of welcome. It literally means, "You're coming is pleasant."

İnşallah: God willing.

ka: In Istanbul Armenian, ka is an expression similar to "hey" in English, but used to address women only.

kaknem: Shitty.

kıbrağ: Diyarbakır slang for pimp.

kirve: The man who restrains a boy during his circumcision.

Lodos: Southwestern wind.

lüfer: bluefish.

Meğa Asdudzo: Good God! (Armenian).

meyhane: Traditional Turkish drinking places.

meze: The special dishes eaten to accompany rakı.

müsü: Although the tradition is gradually disappearing, Armenians use this term (from the French, Monsieur) before the first name as a term of respect. Women also use this term when speaking about their husbands.

rakı: Popular in Turkey, rakı is an alcoholic drink, the most potent ingredient of which is anice.

Selamünaleykümüne: Arabic greeting.

simit: A doughnut-shaped bread covered with toasted sesame seeds.

Teyze: Literally, "maternal aunt," it is commonly used as a term of respect for women older than oneself.

vay, vay vay: like "my, my, my"

zo: Rough slang for "guy/man" (Armenian).